...~~thi~~n thread of control
...~~he~~ backed her up against
...~~wall~~ of the club. When her fingers
pulled ~~him~~ out, it tore a groan from him. He
kissed her lips, her eyes, then he twined his
fingers through her hair and tugged her head
back to feast on her neck. *More*, he thought,
and he slid up her short skirt to find only skin,
only her, slick, swollen and ready.

"Sabrina," he breathed, and it took everything
he had to keep himself from letting go…not
until his fingers were on her, not until he was
in her, not until he felt her come.

The huge TV screen suspended above the bar,
constantly flashed images of the room. One
man sent a woman writhing with every stroke
of his tongue. On the dance floor, a couple
discreetly fondled each other.

And in the corner, Sabrina, wrapped around
Stef, impaled on him, braced against the wall,
released ~~a shudder~~...

Dear Reader,

Welcome to my new trilogy, SEX & THE
SUPPER CLUB. Sabrina, Kelly, Trish, Cilla,
Paige, Thea and Delaney met during college
when they were all working on a drama
production. The bonds they formed were strong,
and even as the years have passed they've
remained entwined in each other's lives through
the weekly dinners of the Sex & the Supper
Club. Over the course of coming books, you'll
get to know them and watch them one by one
conquer the challenges in their lives and find
true love.

I grew up in the LA area, while my sister still
lives there. We've done a lot of hard work
scouting locations – you should see how we
suffered having to go to all these wonderful
restaurants, hip bars and other hot spots. The
things I do for love… Speaking of which, I hope
you enjoy reading Stef and Sabrina's love story.
Drop me a line at kristin@kristinhardy.com and
tell me what you think. Or visit my website at
www.kristinhardy.com for contests, recipes and
updates on my recent and upcoming releases.

Have fun,

Kristin Hardy

TURN ME ON

BY
KRISTIN HARDY

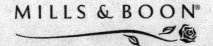

MILLS & BOON®

To Gretchen,
who runs with a fast crowd,
and to Stephen,
always and forever.

Hardy, Kristin

Turn me on /
Kristin Hardy

ROM Pbk

1833275

MILLS & BOON and MILLS & BOON with the Rose Device
are registered trademarks of the publisher.

First published in Great Britain 2006
by Harlequin Mills & Boon Limited, Eton House,
18-24 Paradise Road,
Richmond, Surrey TW9 1SR

© Kristin Lewotsky 2004

ISBN 0 263 84580 X

14-0106

Printed and bound in Spain
by Litografía Rosés S.A., Barcelona

Prologue

Big Drama Behind the Scenes
Kelly Vandervere, staff writer
Daily Californian

When it comes to drama, the play's the thing. It's not just about acting, though. If it weren't for a crew of dedicated behind-the-scenes volunteers, the drama department's spring 1996 production of Shakespeare's *Henry V* would never see the light of day.

Dialogue is key, which is why Trish Dawson and her collaborators from the English deaprtment have spent many hours trimming the script to fit a two-hour college production. It's not all words, though. *Henry V* also in-cludes dramatic battle scenes choreographed by dance major Thea Mitchell.

And the production has to look right. Design major Cilla Danforth supervises wardrobe, coming up with au-thentic-looking period costumes from the drama depart-ment's archives. Paige Wheeler, also from the design department, complements Danforth's work with gorgeous set decoration that evokes the medieval era.

Of course, all that hard work wouldn't mean anything

without the clever marketing campaign of business major Delaney Phillips. And to make sure the production is recorded for posterity, film major Sabrina Pantolini is capturing it in a video documentary.

So when you're in your seats tonight enjoying the premiere of the production, applaud the actors but don't forget to clap a few times for all the other folks who make the magic happen.

1

"WHAT I WANT FROM YOU, honey, is sex." Royce Schuyler, the Home Cinema vice president of programming, stared across the restaurant table to where Sabrina Pantolini sat—poised, sleek and dark like a silky cat. "You give me that, and everything else will follow."

"Royce, honey, I'll give you the best sex you've ever had." Sabrina smiled, her eyes ripe with promise and fun. A golden topaz hung winking from a gold chain around her neck. "This documentary series is going to have people stopping to take cold showers."

"Swingers are old hat. Don't give me swingers."

Sabrina snorted and pushed her short, dark hair back behind her ears. "Forget swingers. That's practically pedestrian. I'm talking about blow job tutors, exhibitionist hotels, you name it. It's perfect for cable—all the stuff that the networks would never have the nerve to touch, and you guys will be putting it right in the late-night living rooms of Middle America."

"With a guarantee like that, I'm looking forward to the pilot."

"Great. Does that mean you're ready to sign on for

it?" Her goat cheese and heirloom tomato salad sat in front of her, forgotten.

Royce shook his head and scanned the restaurant with a practiced eye. "Not yet. I want to see what you've got when you finish the pilot."

"I need working capital, Royce."

"I'm sure you do, but I can't give it to you." He took a drink of his seltzer water. "Right now, you've got no track record and no staff on board."

Sabrina suppressed a surge of annoyance. The money she was asking for was chump change for a cable network like Home Cinema and Schuyler knew it. On the other hand, she was fortunate he was even here talking to her. If she'd been anyone else, she'd have been lucky to meet some mid-level flunky in the city offices. Instead, she was here talking with Home Cinema's vice president of programming in a see-and-be-seen restaurant.

She had no illusions about why she was getting the VIP treatment. Her father, Michael Pantolini, had been the kind of director people talked about in hushed whispers. Even five years after his death in an auto accident, Sabrina was still connected to the Hollywood power structure through her producer uncle, her action-star cousin and her set-designer mother. Sabrina was Hollywood royalty, but if it gave her some small edge, it also made her chafe.

"I can make a better pilot if I have Home Cinema behind me," she said in a slightly bored voice, waving across the room to an actress she knew slightly.

"Find a way to make a hot pilot on your own. That's the mark of a good producer. Bring it to me and we'll talk." Royce took a sip of his drink. "Hey, isn't that your cousin who just came in?"

Sabrina glanced over at the door where Matt Ramsay had just arrived with this month's hot starlet on his arm. Oh yeah, she knew how this worked. Royce expected her to call Matt over and introduce them. It would up Royce's collateral with everyone in the room to be seen talking to the big box-office hero. And maybe the next time Royce was looking to cast an action miniseries, he'd have a better chance of getting Matt. Sabrina stifled a sigh. Sometimes she found the treacly, sycophantic side of Hollywood almost impossible to tolerate.

If she were smart, she'd use Matt to work Royce and get her funding. That was how it was done in Hollywood. Sabrina wasn't always smart that way, though. She had a feisty disposition as classically Italian as the arc of her cheekbones, her vivid coloring and the hollows of her eyelids that somehow lent an extra importance to her every expression. She didn't want to use her family connections to make this happen. She wanted to make *True Sex* fly on its own. If she could have gotten away with it, she'd have used her mother's name. Unfortunately, Sabrina Pantolini was far too well-known from her years in the media spotlight to work incognito.

Matt waved and started over to where she sat.

Sabrina sighed. "All right, Schuyler, I'll get you your pilot in six weeks. You like it, you give me a series contract." She rose. "Thanks for lunch."

"SO ARE YOU AN AUNTIE YET, Laeticia?" Sabrina asked her assistant as she breezed into the office of Pantolini

Productions. Offices, really, if you counted the tiny reception/waiting area as separate from the cramped room behind it. Though her offices were tucked in an old building off Hollywood Boulevard instead of in Westwood, they were hers. Besides, they were big enough in a town where all the important meetings took place in restaurants.

"An auntie? Not so far. My sister's taking her time. Of course, that girl's been late for everything since her own birth, so it doesn't surprise me a bit." Laeticia was long and slender, with gorgeous, mocha-colored skin and doe-soft eyes. When they'd met, Sabrina had wondered how a woman like Laeticia could possibly take on the production coordinator's role of logistics, paperwork and organization, let alone survive the Hollywood meat grinder. To her surprise, the woman was ruthlessly efficient, able to alternately sweet-talk and bully as the situation demanded. Anyone who underestimated Laeticia did so at his peril.

"Patience. You know what they say about watched pots."

"Mmmm. So how did the meeting go with the brass?"

Sabrina moved her shoulders noncommittally. "Well enough, I suppose. They want to see more. Now we just have to deliver."

"That doesn't sound too hard."

Sabrina made a face at her. "Any messages or mail?"

"Your new cell phone is here," Laeticia said, handing her a small box. "I activated it for you. Try not to lose this one, hmmm?"

Sabrina grinned. "You're a lifesaver."

Laeticia picked up a pair of small pink notes. "Gus Stirling called to remind you that the night shoot on the *Hollywood Hauntings* project has moved to the Sunset Boulevard location."

Augustus Stirling, Sabrina's godfather and teacher. The thought of seeing him made her smile, though with the night shoot he had planned, they'd probably go until the sun was coming up. No sleep for her tonight, she thought resignedly. The fact that in her partying days she'd seldom arrived home before breakfast didn't make her any happier about missing her slumber. Back then, she'd crash until three or four in the afternoon if she'd felt like it. Now, she had to rise and shine early in the morning to meet deadlines and get work done.

But Gus had taken her seriously when she'd decided she wanted to work in film and had taught her the job from the ground up. He'd been tough on her, forcing her to prove herself again and again. He wasn't shy about working her hard and she'd be damned if she'd stop a second before he did.

"You also had a call from Kelly Vandervere, reminding you that the Supper Club is at Gilbert's at seven."

Nachos, margaritas and gossip with old friends. Sabrina's mouth curved into an arc of pleasure. That much, at least, would make the rest of the night tolerable. "And?"

"Just remember, don't get too worn out tonight. If Kisha goes into labor later, I might be coming in late tomorrow."

Sabrina winked at her. "Here's hoping I'm on my own and you're an auntie."

"Just what I need—baby-sitting and diaper-changing duties," Laeticia muttered, but her eyes held a smile as she said it.

FIVE HOURS LATER, Sabrina opened the glass door of Gilbert's and stepped into a bar area filled with the sound of blenders. It seemed as if half her time was spent in restaurants, she thought wryly as she passed the hostess stand with a nod. Then she turned the corner and spied the group of women seated at a table, talking animatedly, half hidden by a lattice. The usual faces.

And the usual discussions.

"Forget all this feel-good stuff. Reality is, size matters," said a tawny-haired woman with an angular face.

"Not true." The words were definite, the speaker dressed in a silky floral op-art blouse from the latest Dolce & Gabbana collection. "Bigger might be better, but it's what he does with it that makes the difference."

The first woman snorted. "Oh, come on, Cilla. The guy's twenty-two," she said, taking a swig of her margarita. "He doesn't know enough to do anything with it. With them, it's just in and out, with maybe a few hours sleep in between. At least if it's big, he's got a fighting chance to do some good."

Sabrina ducked around the corner. "On the other hand, there's a limit to size. It has to be big enough for basic purposes, but too much beyond that it just hurts."

Six sets of eyes stared at her blankly.

"Sabrina? Good to see you, sweetie, but what the hell do you mean?" asked the tawny-haired woman, Kelly Vandervere.

Sabrina pulled up a chair at the table and signaled to the waiter for a beer. "Come on, admit it. We've all had to groan through getting pounded by some guy who thinks a monster boner and an ability to recite batting averages in his head is all he needs to send a woman to heaven. Size isn't everything." She speared a pickled jalapeño out of the bowl on the table.

"What are you talking about?" asked Cilla Danforth, an amused frown on her triangular, foxy-looking face.

It was Sabrina's turn to look blank. "Tackle. Aren't you?"

Laughter rose around her. "Apartments," said Kelly, wiping her eyes. "We were talking about my little brother's new apartment. Only someone with your filthy mind would think we were talking about dicks."

"Sorry. It was the thought of all your dirty minds that made me assume you were talking about sex," Sabrina said with dignity, taking her beer from the waiter. "So if you're not talking about it, does that mean that nobody's getting it?"

"Do you guys realize we've talked about sex every single week for the past five years? You're obsessed. Let's do something else for a change." Dark-haired Thea Mitchell, dressed in her perpetual black, scooped up salsa with a chip and crunched it.

Cilla and Kelly looked at each other. "I like talking about sex," Kelly offered.

"Yeah. It's the next best thing to having it," tossed in Delaney Phillips, a corn-silk blonde in a candy-pink lace camisole and a black choker. "I bet you'd change your tune if we just set you up with a man. We could do Trish, too, while we're at it."

"No way." With her curly red hair skinned back from her face and no makeup, Trish almost managed to disguise her gorgeous bone structure. "I'm on dating sabbatical, remember? That's why I hang out with you guys—to live vicariously."

"Well, *somebody's* got to be getting it." Sabrina looked around the table.

"Possibly," Cilla said. "Paige had a date the other night, I know, because she wouldn't go to the gym with me."

Cool and patrician, Paige gave a graceful shrug. "Nothing much to tell. He was just my escort to a fund-raiser."

Five heads around the table perked up. "Spill it," Kelly demanded.

Paige shook her head and the blond layers of her expensive haircut swished and settled perfectly. "His name is Landon, and—"

"That should have sent you running right there," Cilla interjected. "Never date a guy with a trust-fund name. I know these guys, Paige. You're just asking for death by boredom."

"Says the trust-fund kid herself," Trish jabbed lightly.

"I don't have a trust fund."

Trish rolled her eyes. "I'm sorry, a chain of department stores."

"The stores belong to my dad." Cilla twisted her chunky amethyst David Yurman cocktail ring. "I'm just a working stiff like the rest of you, remember? Anyway, we're not talking about me. The guy sounds like a preppster. Where did he grow up, Paige?"

"Greenwich, Connecticut."

"I rest my case," Cilla said smugly.

"He was nice enough. Smart, well-informed." She paused while the waitress set plates of quesadillas in front of them. "Good job in the legal department at Fox."

"Yeah, yeah, yeah." Delaney wrinkled her snub nose. "Get to the good stuff. How did he kiss?"

Paige aimed a chilly look at Delaney, who merely grinned.

"Give it up, Paige. We've seen you cleaning the bathroom in your underwear."

The cool look evaporated and Paige laughed. "I knew I was out of my mind when I moved in with you guys back then."

"Are you kidding? We taught you how to have a good time. Now tell us about the kiss," Kelly ordered.

Paige eyed them. "Too wet. Too much tongue, too quickly."

"Sounds like a first kiss," Thea muttered, taking a sip of her iced tea.

"Was that how your first kiss was?" Cilla asked her. "That's too bad. Mine was pretty good. Jason Stilton, third grade."

"Third grade?" Paige raised an eyebrow.

"He was precocious," Cilla said.

"Or someone was," Delaney said. "I didn't get my first kiss until eighth grade. "Jake Gordon, boyfriend number one." She sighed a little dreamily.

"I don't remember the name of my first kiss, but I bet the location's got you all beat," Kelly wagered.

"I'll bite," Sabrina said. "Where?"

"On the Matterhorn at Disneyland."

"The Matterhorn?" Sabrina reached out for a slice of quesadilla. "You know the make-out ride was the Haunted Mansion."

"Hey, you take what you can get when you can get it."

Delaney snorted. "And when can you get it on the Matterhorn? Try it there, you lose some teeth."

"You know the part where you're getting pulled up the first hill? My girlfriend and I had met him and his buddy in line, so he was sitting behind me in the bobsled. I leaned back to say something to him and wham, full tongue and everything."

"Nothing like jumping in at the deep end," Trish said.

"Shocked the heck out of me. I was thirteen. I thought kissing was about lips. Then we got to the top of the hill and the ride started."

"You didn't keep kissing, did you?"

"God no. We'd have dislocated our necks, or at least lost our tongues."

"Well, I don't know about the first kiss, but my best kiss is still Carl Reynolds, that guy I dated last year," said Cilla, reaching out for a pickled carrot.

"I thought you said he was a waste of a human being," Paige objected.

"Oh, he was. But he was still a great kisser," Cilla said.

"My best kisser was the guy I went out with last week, I think," Kelly threw in. "Of course, that's always subject to change," she said with an appraising glance around the room. "What about you, Sabrina?"

"What, best kiss or first kiss?"

"Best kiss. First kiss is too easy."

Sabrina took a thoughtful drink of her beer and set it down. "Stef Costas, the first time we kissed."

"Definite waste of a human being," Kelly said decisively.

"But a great kisser."

SABRINA OPENED HER PURSE and pulled out a couple of bills to toss on the table. "Okay, that's all for me."

Delaney stared at her. "It's only nine-thirty."

"I've got a night shoot starting in an hour," she explained.

"A night shoot?" Kelly might have worked for *Hot Ticket* magazine for her day job, but as near as Sabrina could tell, she was never off shift.

"For the Hollywood ghost documentary. We're going to the *Château Mirabelle,* where Elaine Chandler overdosed. Supposedly there's a cold spot in her room and guests who've stayed there swear they've seen an apparition."

"Brrr. That's creepy," Trish said with a grimace.

"Don't tell me you believe in ghosts." Kelly gave her an amused glance.

"I'm not so cynical that I don't believe there are things out there we don't understand."

"Hah. You just pretend to be a cynic. Deep inside, you're a mushy romantic," Kelly corrected, pulling her plate forward with relish. "I'm the cynic. Forget about Mr. Right. Me, I'll settle for Mr. Right Now. It's a lot less trouble," she said, eyeing the waiter speculatively. "What I don't believe, Sabrina, is that you, with your multimillion-dollar trust fund, are playing the working schlep. In your shoes, I'd quit in a minute."

Trish broke in. "You are so full of it. You'd report for *Hot Ticket* for free and you know it. Where else would you have official license to poke into things that don't concern you?"

Kelly ran her tongue around her teeth. "Okay, guilty as charged. But seriously, Sabrina, why work so hard if you don't have to?"

"You know why. I want to work for myself."

"So do it. You've got the bankroll," Paige pointed out, patting her mouth with her napkin and setting it on the table.

"That's my family's money, not mine. Plus I don't have the know-how, or at least I didn't. You know the deal I made with Uncle Gus—I work, he teaches."

"But you have worked," Trish protested.

"She's right, Rina," Thea said mildly. "You've been at this for almost five years. Whatever happened to that idea you were talking about for a cable documentary?"

Should she say something or would she jinx herself? "Funny you should ask," Sabrina began, a ridiculously broad grin spreading across her face. "I'm just about ready to start shooting."

A chorus of congratulations erupted around the table.

"What does your family think?" asked Cilla, who knew a thing or two about family legacies, having grown up in her father's retail empire.

Sabrina slanted her a dry look. "You know what my family thinks," she said. "That I'll give it up sooner or later for a party." She permitted herself a mischievous smile. "Or at least that's what they'd think if they didn't know the topic of the documentary. If they did, they might be a little less than thrilled."

"What is the topic?" Paige asked, curious.

Sabrina pursed her lips. "Kinky sex, of course."

Kelly hooted. "Tame, Pantolini. Show me a film that's not about sex."

"Wait till you see this one," Sabrina promised, eyes alight with fun. "Sex clubs, exhibitionists in the act, blow job tutorials. Tonight's my last night working for somebody else. Come tomorrow, I get rolling on *True Sex,* coming soon to a cable station near you."

2

SABRINA SAT IN A cast-iron chair on the patio of her Uncle Gus's Hollywood Hills bungalow, eyes closed and head tipped back in the warm afternoon sunlight. The night shoot had gone smoothly, but the loss of sleep was beginning to catch up with her. That, and anxiety over the bombshell that had been dropped in her lap that morning. She wouldn't think about it for a few minutes, though. For a few minutes, she'd just relax and not fret about deadlines or logistics.

Or the fact that her director had skipped to a different project.

The sound of the sliding glass door had her raising her head to see Gus step onto the flagstone patio, two glasses of iced tea in his hands. Though he was closing in on the age most people started drawing Social Security, time hadn't stooped him or stiffened his easy stride. Maybe the years had added a network of lines to his hawk face and silvered the hair that flowed down over his collar, but, if anything, the changes made him appear even more wise, even more filled with the answers.

Answers she currently needed very badly.

He sat, staring at her with a faint smile on his face.

"What?" Sabrina asked.

"I'm just remembering you at your christening, kicking and squalling at the top of your lungs. You've grown up nicely."

Sabrina gave him a tired smile. "Sometimes I don't feel grown-up at all. At least, not grown-up enough to do everything that needs doing."

He set a glass in front of her. "If it's worth doing, it's rarely easy."

She nodded.

"How did your meeting with Schuyler go?"

Sabrina took a sip of her tea. "It went well, I think. He likes the concept. I played him on the competition with Spotlight! and he jumped."

"What did you walk away with?"

"He's open to it. All we have to do is wow him with the pilot and we're home free."

Gus nodded, watching a hummingbird whisk around the feeder that hung from the eaves of the house. "Well, that puts your foot in the door."

"Yeah." She rubbed her temples. "Except I just lost my director."

Gus snapped his head around to stare at her. "I thought he was locked in."

"He'd done everything but ink the papers," she said, resisting the urge to begin pacing. "Timing's everything in this business, you know that. Someone else offered him something he liked better."

"So what are you going to do, kid?"

Sabrina gave him a wry smile. "I thought you might

ask that. I spent the afternoon beating the bushes to find out who's available and who I could afford."

"And?"

"And nothing. I called everyone I could think of. No one's free, at least no one who could do what we need." She squared her shoulders. "I'll do some more calling tomorrow. I can't lose time when I've already told Schuyler it's coming."

Gus stroked his chin. "Did you try Marcus Amblin?"

Sabrina nodded. "No dice."

"Petra Krausz?"

"Ditto. And Lloyd Asherton and the Lamonte-Crosby group. Everyone's got balls in the air," she finished morosely, rubbing patterns in the condensation on her glass. "Doesn't mean it's not going to happen eventually, it's just that the delay makes me look bad to Schuyler."

Gus tapped his fingers on the table. "There's one possibility I can think of," he said slowly. "Someone who owes me a favor and might be willing to help us out. You'd probably only have him for the pilot, but that'll buy you some time to find another director for the main series. First things first, after all."

Sabrina shook her head. "I don't want you to call in favors on my account. I need to do this myself."

"Oh, trust me, you'll do it yourself. I'm just going to see if I can help clear the path a little."

"Advice only, remember? And a swift kick in the pants if I ever need one. I don't want you coming in and smoothing things over for me, Gus."

Humor crinkled the corners of his eyes. "Trust me, petunia, if this works out, smooth is the last thing it'll be."

She gave him a suspicious look before raising her glass to take a sip. "What have you got up your sleeve? Who are you talking about?"

"He's a filmmaker's filmmaker," he told her. "He's not always easy, but he's talented."

"Who, Gus?" she persisted.

"He'll be the one to take your concept from interesting to sublime."

"Gus." Her voice was full of warning.

The edge of his mouth twitched with what she could have sworn was humor. "Stef Costas."

The glass of tea slipped from her fingers and shattered on the pavement.

STEFOS COSTAS SLOUCHED in front of the editing machine, scanning the black-and-white film of striking workers that flickered on the screen in front of him. The picket line stood blocking an old-fashioned factory gate, the men looking shabby and grimly determined. Then a jet of water shot in, knocking the men down. Stef frowned and stopped the film, rolling it back to review a few seconds' worth of footage. At his elbow, the phone jangled for attention, but he ignored it, moving the film slowly, looking for the moment…there, that was it—the frame in which the first man was hit by the water, grimacing as the jet sent him tumbling over.

Stef's straight dark hair fell over his forehead. He shoved it impatiently out of his way, pressing the editing controls to make the new cut and splice it into an interview with a historian. The room's faint light turned his cheekbones into sharp slashes below eyes that were nearly black. He studied the new edit, the intensity that drew his face taut now softening slightly in satisfaction.

In film circles, Stef was known as a gifted documentary director. Focused, even driven, some said, he was the genius behind a critically lauded film about espionage in the American War of Independence and one on the Industrial Revolution. Unfortunately, being a hot property in documentary circles didn't necessarily bring in cash or translate into getting green-lighted on any project he wished, not when he was crafting cinematic releases. Unless you were Ken Burns with a big-money sponsor and a main line to PBS, getting docs funded was always a battle. Fortunately, his next project—his dream project—was all set, just as soon as he finished his current piece on the early union movement.

It was time for him to make a film that really engaged him again. Of late, he'd been going through the motions. Sure, he was satisfied with his craftsmanship, but somehow it wasn't quite enough to get rid of the restlessness that niggled at him.

When the phone jangled again, he reached over absently and picked it up.

"Costas," he said economically, eyes on the screen as he fast-forwarded the film to reach his next target segment.

"Stef? Mitch." It was the voice of his producer. "How's it going?"

"Good. I'm finishing the edits on the union piece. I made a contact in Athens who's going to fast-track some of the permit and approvals process. With luck, seven weeks from now, yours truly will be on the coast of the Aegean, filming." And witnessing the excavation of a

World War II execution site that held clues to the fates of members of the Greek underground. Members who might, perhaps, have included his grandfather.

If he closed his eyes, Stef could hear his grandmother's heavily accented English as she told his younger self the stories of what had happened, what little she knew. And she'd wept. Even then, as a child, he'd vowed to ferret out the true story, to someday be able to tell her what had happened to the man she'd loved. The rift that had subsequently opened between her and his career-obsessed parents when she'd criticized their child-rearing hadn't weakened his ties to her or the strength of his determination.

For years, Stef had researched the topic, waiting for the right moment to dive in. With two award-winning films already under his belt and the hotly anticipated union doc scheduled to premiere in a month, the timing felt right. "Everything's looking good on this end as far as prep goes. I talked with the university team today, and they're ready to have me film the entire excavation process."

"Uh, can you get an extension on that?"

Stef's expression sharpened. "Why?" He stopped the editing machine. "What's going on, Mitch?"

There was a pause. "Atkinson and Trimax are backing out. Maybe it's a cash-flow thing, but they're not prepared to go forward until the next fiscal year at the earliest."

Stef cursed. "You know my window's limited. They're going to dig up this site whether I'm there or not, and once it's done, it's done." He stood and paced across the room. "We've been talking with these guys for three years. They know the parameters of the project. What are they doing dropping out now?"

"Everyone's skittish in this economy."

"Have you tried the indie studios?"

Mitch let out a sigh. "I've been burning up the phones all day. No one wants to bite. Not now. People want feel-good movies, date movies. Cinematic docs are never easy, you know that."

"Did you try the foundations?" Stef demanded, raking a hand through his hair while he calculated how much money he might be able to scare up in grants.

"No dice. Look, Stef, they're not backing out, it's just a delay. You were planning to work on the piece about that Rhode Island nightclub fire after you got through in Greece, right? So swap the order, do Rhode Island first and Greece after. It'll work out. You've just got to be patient."

"I *am* being patient, Mitch," Stef said ominously. "The university group is starting their dig in two months. A year from now, they're going to be done."

"I'm being conservative with the twelve to eighteen months, Stef. It could happen sooner."

"Even six months is too late."

"Look, I'm not going to fight with you." Mitch paused. "Finish up the union film, take a couple of months off and you can start Rhode Island. We can use that to fund Greece, if you need to. You can work with the still photos they'll take during the excavation. You've always had a genius for that."

"Thanks for the vote of confidence."

Mitch sighed. "You've been waiting a decade to do this. What's another year?"

It was the difference between crucial footage and telling a dead story, Stef wanted to roar. It was squandering a golden opportunity to tell the story he wanted, the only story that really mattered to him.

Instead, he held on to his control. "Look, Mitch, keep the pressure on them. And do me a favor—don't stop looking."

Stef hung up the phone and stood for a moment. Then he kicked his chair and sent it spinning in circles. Against the wall, grainy black-and-white footage showed a frame of union men pelting scabs with rocks.

The phone rang again, and this time he picked it up with a snarl. "Costas."

"You've got a bark on you, boy. Gus Stirling here. Got a minute?"

Stef's face relaxed. "Gus. It's good to hear your voice. How've you been?"

"Good. I hear your union piece is supposed to premiere next month."

Stef glanced at the screen. "Assuming I finish the edit."

"You always were a perfectionist. Did my cousin at the Greek Film Commission take care of you?"

"He was a godsend. Pushed through all the permits in record time. I owe him one. You, too."

"I didn't do anything much, it was all Louie. He's a good man to know."

"I'll say. What can I do to thank him?"

Gus chuckled. "Buy him a glass of ouzo when you get to Athens. He'll like that."

"Consider it done, assuming I ever get over there."

"What do you mean? I thought you said the permits came through."

Frustration started to simmer again in Stef's blood. "They did. Unfortunately, there's been a holdup in funding. Hopefully not long, but it looks like I won't be going over for a couple of months, at least."

"So what are you going to do when your union piece is done?"

Stef shrugged, forgetting Gus couldn't see him. "I don't know, preproduction? A vacation? Set up on a street corner and beg for money?"

Gus snorted. "If I know you, preproduction was done six months ago, and you've never taken a vacation in all the time I've known you. And you never beg."

"Maybe it's time I started. They're excavating a key site over there in about eight weeks. If I miss that, I miss the heart of the doc." And he missed the chance to pick up a clue about his grandfather, he thought. "I've got to find a way to go, and until I do, I can't really get into anything serious."

"Sure you can, if it's small enough."

This wasn't just a social call, Stef realized suddenly, staring at the flickering black-and-white footage on the wall. "What's on your mind, Gus?"

He could hear the smile in the older man's voice. "That obvious, huh? I used to be better at this."

"That's the problem with getting in the habit of shooting straight with someone. You tend to lose the art of B.S."

"A symptom of my advancing age, no doubt. Well, let me just cut to the chase. I could help you out with your funding problems. As you know, I'm the head of a little consortium that funds a couple of small films a year. Though, I've got a little problem to take care of before I can really afford to think about that."

Here it came, Stef thought. "And that would be?"

Gus coughed. "I've got a project that needs a director. The person scheduled to do it ducked out unexpectedly, and the shooting's supposed to start next week."

Something had Stef's radar going haywire. "What is it?"

"Cable documentary, a one-hour pilot."

"What's the topic?"

"It's an alternative lifestyles thing."

"You mean sex," Stef said flatly.

"Sex," Gus agreed.

His first inclination was to say hell no, but the prospect of being able to get his Greek documentary off the ground had him pausing. "Who's the producer?"

"She's new to the game, but I've been teaching her the ropes the past few years. I think you'll find her tough and fair."

"Who, Gus?"

"My goddaughter, Sabrina Pantolini."

Like an icy wave, memories swamped him and robbed him of breath. Laughing eyes, a mouth always curved up in some sort of devilment, a body greedy for his touch. Eight years before, when he'd been in grad school, Sabrina Pantolini had been his lover.

Eight years before, she'd been his love.

Film had been what he'd lived and breathed, the drive for success pumping through his veins. Still, even he wasn't immune to a woman like Sabrina. She'd taught him about life beyond film, brought him out into the fresh air. Taught him what it was like to love and be loved.

And she had taught him about betrayal.

"Oh, come on Gus, you know better than to ask something like this. A sex documentary is bad enough, but with *her?*"

"She's grown up a lot, Stef. She's serious about this."

"This week."

"And the week before, and the five years before that," Gus said reprovingly. "She's paid her dues and been part of some damned fine work. I should know—she's been doing it for me."

How was it that he hadn't known about this, Stef asked himself. He certainly hadn't missed her face in any of the glossy newsstand magazines. She unveiled a new grand career every week, or so it seemed, in between showing up at the hot parties with some good-looking guy on her arm. Not that that bothered him, he thought, loosening his jaw. The past was the past.

And he hadn't exactly been celibate himself, not that any of them had stuck. There had been other women, but none who felt right in his arms, none who tasted right. None who had been able to make him laugh and feel truly light the way Sabrina had. First love, he told himself, just memories of first love.

"Look, Stef, I realize what I'm asking here. The question is do you want to do your Greek doc or don't you? If you want it, then it's a trade-off. I'll get you the money and you get me that pilot in the can. Four weeks is all I'm asking."

"Plus postproduction," Stef reminded him.

"Plus postproduction, but that will go quicker than you think."

Stef hesitated. Gus was right; he didn't beg, and somehow taking money from a friend seemed like the same thing.

"You've got me in a bind here, Gus."

"Nonsense." Gus's voice was brisk. "I'm offering you a way out. And you'll be doing me that favor you said you owed me."

Stef rubbed his temple. It was imperative that he get to Greece while the excavation was still going on. He owed it to his grandfather to tell his story the right way; he owed it to himself and his family to find out what he could.

Besides, maybe before he uncovered one part of his past, he could bury another—the image he held of Sabrina from days gone by. Maybe, he thought, just maybe it would be good for him to take on Gus's project. Reality couldn't possibly match up to the memory. He'd see her, talk with her, get her out of his head once and for all.

And when he was done with the project, he'd be done with her.

"I'll do it," Stef said suddenly.

"Wonderful." Gus's voice was delighted. "I'll get some numbers from your producer and we can move things along. As far as the cable doc…" he paused.

"It's as good as done," Stef said, ignoring his bellyful of misgivings at the idea of working with Sabrina again.

Yeah, he was sure it was just misgivings.

3

"WHAT DO YOU MEAN, I have to have a fire truck on site?" Sabrina demanded of the faceless bureaucrat on the phone. "It's not like we're setting and filming open fires in the middle of a national forest. We're filming on a street."

She sighed, tapping a pen on the stack of forms in front of her. She knew the cycle of permit after permit after permit by heart. That didn't mean she had to like it. Sometimes, the regulations made sense. More often, she suspected they were put into place merely to torment her.

"All right," she said, giving in to the inevitable. "Off-duty cops and an off-duty fire truck on site at all times. If we get that, are we good to go?" At the affirmative answer, she gave a decisive nod. "Thanks for your help," she said insincerely and hung up the phone.

At the burble and whir of the fax machine in the outer office, Sabrina glanced out her door at Laeticia's empty desk—Kisha had finally gone into labor and Laeticia was with her, leaving Sabrina to fend for herself. Just what she needed. Bad enough she was facing the prospect of dealing with Stef Costas again; now her office routine was falling apart. She was a professional, though. She'd deal with the office and she'd sure as hell deal with Stef. He might have mowed her over at nineteen, not now.

Frowning at herself, Sabrina began to update her scheduling software with a list of shoots. A roving New York sex club, a lap dance tutor, a hotel for exhibitionists…Home Cinema wouldn't know what had hit it. A lot of babies would be born nine months after the premiere, she thought, a broad smile spreading across her face.

Two years of being a production manager had made Sabrina an expert in problem-solving, but that didn't mean it was pleasant. Laeticia made the office an oasis of sanity and order; Sabrina felt her absence keenly. The phone rang and Sabrina snatched it up, only to find a telemarketer on the other end. A raise, she thought as she hung up. Laeticia definitely deserved a raise.

Sabrina made a noise of frustration at the peremptory blat of sound in the reception room. The fax machine had gone silent; it didn't take a genius to put two and two together. With a sigh, Sabrina rose to take care of it. The signed contract for the documentary was coming through and the last thing she needed was to run out of paper in the middle of it.

She pulled open the doors of the metal cabinet that housed their office supplies. The only box of paper was unopened, which meant digging out Laeticia's box cutter. Bumping her head on an upper shelf, she cursed just as she heard a noise behind her.

"You ought to be more careful, rushing into things like that. Then again, that always was your problem."

Sabrina froze. The words vibrated in the silence of

the room and shivered into the marrow of her bones. Slowly, she straightened up and turned, pushing the hair out of her eyes.

Stef Costas leaned against the wall just inside the door to her office. It snatched the breath from her lungs to see him there. A day-old beard darkened his jaw, framing his mouth. How she'd loved that mouth, addictive and enticing, hot and demanding on hers. How she'd loved him, once upon a time.

Once upon a time…the beginning of all good fairy tales. Theirs had been the fairy story of all time, a magical fantasy of true love.

Only they hadn't lived happily ever after.

She concentrated on the memory, searching for composure. "Well, if it isn't the famous Stef Costas." She gave him a leisurely, intentionally insolent survey. It had been eight years since she'd seen him, aside from the nights he haunted her dreams. The years had stripped down his face to the sharp, tight lines of jaw and cheekbone, the black slashes of brow above midnight eyes, a sheaf of ebony hair hanging over his forehead. His was a face that conjured up thoughts of Alexander the Great, or Jason and the Argonauts. He'd grown leaner, tougher-looking and even more handsome, if that were possible. And, judging by the lack of a wedding ring, free of entanglements.

Stef gave her a mocking stare in return with those black, damn-you-to-the-devil eyes. "And if it isn't the latest Pantolini producer."

"Producer," she repeated slowly, savoring the taste on her tongue. "I believe that makes me your boss, doesn't it?" She saw a quick flash in his eyes before he banked it back. He still had a temper, that much was clear.

"The way I understood it, you were short a director. Let's not forget I'm here doing you a favor—boss," he said.

He also still had that annoying sense of superiority. "I don't need a favor." Her words were brisk, with a note of warning. "What I need is someone who can bring this documentary in on time, within budget and with the look and style I want. As long as we understand each other, we'll do fine."

His eyes were direct, with, she swore, a hint of enjoyment. "Yes, ma'am. Just one thing—we work with my director of photography."

"I've already got a cameraman under contract."

"Pay him off."

"Perhaps you didn't hear what I just said. We're doing this on budget. My guy stays."

"No. Gus tells me you've worked with him on docs before, so you know how these things go. It's one hundred percent intuitive, and you better get the shot right the first time, particularly when it's live action. We don't have the time—and I don't have the patience—to break in a new cameraman." He folded his arms across his chest. "I've been working with Kevin for seven years, he knows how I think. I don't work without him."

She'd dealt with cocky directors before. What was it about Stef that made her want to get in his face and match him attitude for attitude? Maybe it was the calm assurance that he'd get his way, or rather, that his way was the only way. If anything, that aura of unshakable confidence that he'd had in college had deepened and ripened with time. Unfortunately, it only made his dark looks even more appealing, she thought, leaning against the edge of Laeticia's desk.

After all these years, Stef Costas was still stubborn, infuriating and just this side of a prima donna. He was also, in all likelihood, right about the cameraman. She could hear Gus's voice now: "Make the maximum use of your resources. Let the talent do their jobs." Stef was undeniably talented. She was damned if she was going to give in to him completely during their first disagreement, though. Do what's necessary, sure, but she had another maxim—begin as you mean to go on.

It was time to set the tone for how this relationship was going to work.

Unlike when they had been lovers.

"Wait here," Sabrina said, rising. "I'll have a look at the budget."

STEF WATCHED SABRINA cross into her office, his eyes following the arrogant sway of her hips. She wore tight, low-slung pants of the kind that half of the women in L.A. seemed to have adopted as a uniform over the past few years. Watching Sabrina, he suddenly understood the point. Her clingy burgundy top didn't quite reach her belt line, just revealing the points of a stag's horn tattoo that stretched across her lower back. He remembered that tattoo, remembered when she'd gotten it, the first in her circle to do so. And he remembered being in bed with her, tracing its pattern with his tongue.

It seemed he could never have enough of her in those

days. He'd been addicted, as hooked as any junkie. He remembered how she'd felt against him, sleek and springy, humming with arousal. No matter what differences they'd had outside of the bedroom, inside it they'd clicked.

If he were honest, curiosity as much as desperation had driven him to agree to Gus's proposal. The memory of Sabrina—her scent, the feel of her skin—had stubbornly remained in his mind. The years took their toll on everyone; he figured it would do him good to see that the bloom had worn off.

Only now, he could see that it hadn't. One look at those deep-set sherry-brown eyes, that cap of sable curls, and it was clear the bloom had only intensified. Like wine distilled into fine cognac, Sabrina's younger self had deepened into something far more intoxicating. When she'd been nineteen, she could stop traffic; now, he guessed, she could stop hearts.

Not his, though. Not any more.

Stef slid down into a chair along the wall and watched her stalk to a filing cabinet and rummage around in a drawer, yanking out a file. She slapped it down on her desk and sat, leaning forward to read it. Practicality had probably driven her to set her desk facing the door, so that she could easily talk to her assistant. It was just coincidence that he was sitting where it also gave him a direct view of her. He wondered if she realized just how plunging the neckline of her top was, revealing the slight cleft of her cleavage.

Outside, the late summer sun shone from a sky of deadened blue. Inside, the radio played softly, a man singing plaintively about going crazy while he looked into his ex-lover's eyes.

THE FIGURES ON THE SHEET in front of her didn't tell Sabrina anything she didn't already know. She'd stashed some extra money here and there to cover the inevitable overruns. If things broke just right, she probably could pay her current cameraman his release fee and still squeak in on budget. But film projects were like unruly children, always running off in unanticipated directions. If Stef Costas wanted his personal cameraman, he was going to have to pay for it himself.

She was going to enjoy telling him that.

Sabrina glanced up and saw him sitting in one of the row of cheap office chairs next to the outer door—one elbow propped up on the backs, his legs stretched out and crossed at the ankles. He leaned his head back and watched her through slitted eyes. What he was thinking, she couldn't say; she'd never been able to.

Except, perhaps, in bed.

She snapped the folder shut to drive the thought from her mind. There was certainly going to be none of that here. This project was her best shot at establishing herself in the business, of being taken seriously as a filmmaker. And that meant Stef would have to take her seriously as well. Scooping up the folder, she stood and walked back out to where he sat.

"Well, boss?" Stef asked mildly, as if he already knew her response.

Sabrina stifled the urge to throw the folder. It would only amuse him. "I'll let you have your cameraman. But you'll need to come up with the kill fee for the one I've got."

Stef's smile faded. "Really? And how do you expect me to do that?"

Now it was Sabrina's turn to smile. "Well, there's your hefty salary…."

"Nonnegotiable," he said flatly.

Sabrina again sat on the edge of Laeticia's desk, a study in affability. "I'm open to suggestions."

"You're the producer. Isn't that your job?"

Do what's necessary for the production, she told herself and let out her breath slowly. "Yes, it's my job, but we're on a shoestring budget and since you've created a problem by demanding your choice of cameraman, I'm expecting you to be a professional and help find a solution."

Stef's eyes sparked with annoyance, but he didn't say anything for a moment. He tapped his fingers restlessly and stared out the window, obviously in thought. "Do you have a gaffer yet?" he asked, finally.

"No, I'm still working to find someone."

"Kev's assistant usually acts as our gaffer, camera assistant and best boy, all in one."

"I hadn't budgeted for a best boy. I didn't figure we'd need to do dolly work."

"You did plan to have a gaffer, though, right? You do know that to film you've got to have someone manage the lights?"

"Yes, Stef, I know that much."

"Well, Mike can rig lights and do any dolly work we need, plus be Kev's camera assistant. The money you save there should be enough to cover the other cameraman."

Much as she hated to admit it, he was probably right. She'd been hoping to make him squirm a little longer. "Fine. Send me the information and I'll check the numbers. If you're right, all we have to do then is start filming and come up with a pilot that sells."

"Doesn't sound too hard."

"Not as long as we deliver what Royce Schuyler expects."

"Gus said it's about sex," Stef said, unperturbed. "How hard can it be? What's your angle? The sexual revolution revisited? Sexual empowerment for women? The new chastity?"

Sabrina moved to Laeticia's chair and permitted herself a small smile. She was going to enjoy this. "Footage of exhibitionist couples in the act? A sex toy factory? Men who do origami with their cocks?" She would have savored watching his jaw drop more if he hadn't looked so damned gorgeous. "Don't tell me I've shocked you, Stef. You used to be made of sterner stuff."

"You've got to be kidding me. You can't put that kind of stuff on TV," he said positively.

"Who said anything about TV? Cable," she enunciated as though for a child. "It's for late-night cable. Have you seen what they run these days? Trust me, this footage will be tame by comparison. It'll just be more interesting because it's the real thing." She pulled a list of topics from the folder and handed it to Stef. "The first shoot is an ex-stripper who has house parties teaching women to lap dance and take it all off for their husbands."

"No way."

"Royce Schuyler was drooling over the idea," she said with relish.

"He couldn't have been drooling too much or you'd have come away with a contract."

"Come on," she snapped. "No one gets a contract for a doc series sight unseen. He liked the concept, though. Bring the wild side to Middle America. It'll be sexy. It'll be fun."

"No. Not just no, but hell no." Stef walked up to brace his hands on the desk and lean in toward her. "You are out of your mind if you think I'm going to have anything to do with this kind of project. I've got backers who would never return my phone calls if they knew about it."

Sabrina leaned back in her chair and reminded herself to keep her cool. "No problem. Walk out. I'll just tell Gus that you're not interested," she said airily. He had to be pretty desperate, she figured, or he wouldn't be in the same room with her. "Of course, he might be a little disappointed to find out you're not going through with your side of the deal."

"It's not a deal, it's a favor."

Sabrina's smile widened. "In Hollywood, it's the same thing, Stef. Of course, I realize that you've always been above…commercial ventures. Cheer up, sugar. It won't sting so much after a while." She rose and leaned toward him to give him a careless, dismissive kiss on the forehead.

It was a mistake.

IT WAS MORE INSTINCT than intention. Without thinking, Stef angled his head to find Sabrina's mouth. To teach her a lesson…to test them both…to show himself that the past was done. He could have given himself any of those reasons. Any of them would have been easier to accept than the possibility that he just wanted to find out if she felt the same.

Then the heat flared through him and he didn't have to wonder any more why he'd done it.

The taste of her flooded him with delight, like the flavor of some decadent, long-denied dessert. It sucked him back through the years to their first kiss, their last kiss and everything in between. Cool and smooth, her lips were slightly parted at first in shock. He heard her soft, smothered sound of surprise and faint protest; then her mouth was avid and hot against his. Sensations blurred, the sultry scent of her rising around him, the silky strands of her hair spilling over his fingers as he framed her face with his hands.

He wanted more, wanted to have her body naked and quaking under his, to see if she still moved the same way, made the same noises. To see if the same things still turned her on. Then he heard her sigh and felt her surrender herself to the moment.

Small sounds were deafening in the tiny room: the stroke of skin, soft exhale of breath. On the radio, a silky guitar line twined over the voice of a man singing about conquering a lover. Sun spilled across them where it came in the window.

And two people stood, caught in a moment that telescoped the years into nothingness.

SABRINA LIFTED A HAND to Stef's hair, running her fingers through it. She struggled to keep a sense of self, but the sensation overwhelmed her. It was as though she'd spent the past eight years trying chair after chair, finding each uncomfortable, and suddenly the words in her mind were *oh, this fits,* as she sank back into it.

Into him.

It had been so long since the touch of a man had felt so right. And such small touches, only the tantalizing brush of lips, the erotic intimacy of a tongue, and featherlight slip of fingertips over her cheek. Smooth, liquid and slow, the pleasure flowed through her. Time and thought receded. There was only the now, with its endless resonances of before.

Then the door slammed back and someone hurtled into the office with a joyous cry.

"It's a boy!" Laeticia stood in the doorway holding out a bottle of champagne, her triumphant expression morphing into shock as she saw Sabrina and Stef jerk apart. "Oh! I'm sorry, I didn't mean to interrupt."

"No, come in. We were just…" Sabrina willed her pulse to steady. It hadn't meant anything, she told herself, just a kiss like any other. The important thing was not to react. She moved swiftly around the desk to pull Laeticia into a hug. "Congratulations, Auntie."

"Yeah, well, I should get out of here."

"Not at all," Sabrina said with a hint of panic, drawing Laeticia into a chair. It gave her time to think, time to remember how absolutely done with Stef she was, had been for years. "I want to hear all about it." And she did, too. "Mr. Costas was just leaving."

"Not quite yet," Stef countered, looking irritatingly unruffled. "We still need to finish that preproduction meeting."

"I thought it was finished. You clearly don't want to make the pilot that I've already pitched to the cable chief. I've got to deliver what he verbally committed to. Guess that means I have to get a different director."

"I'm your director," he said flatly.

"Not if you don't want to make the documentary I'm selling."

"Don't forget the contract." He nodded toward the fax machine where Laeticia was unobtrusively changing the paper.

"The contract just says we work together on a pilot. Period."

Stef looked at her, amused. "Excuse us," he said to Laeticia, and pulled Sabrina into her office, closing the door.

"Don't manhandle me," she spat.

"I'm not. I'm just trying to get some privacy. We have a contract to work on this project together," he said calmly.

"Fine." An edge entered Sabrina's voice. "Then we do it my way."

"No," Stef shook his head, "we do it our way."

"And what way is that? You were never much good at compromises, Stef."

"Neither were you," he said, looking at her stubborn jaw. "Looks like this will be a learning experience for both of us."

Sabrina took a step closer to him, eyes defiant. "The

first thing you should learn is not to assume that anything you once knew still applies. I'm not a teenager anymore."

"No," he agreed, running his gaze over her, "you're all grown-up."

"And I've grown out of a lot of things. I've found my focus."

"And that is?"

"Making provocative entertainment."

"It didn't take growing up to teach you how to be provocative," he said, lifting a hand toward her cheek. "I think you had that from the day you were born."

Sabrina took a sudden, quick breath and backed away from him. "I grew out of something else in the last eight years, Stef."

"What?"

"You." She opened the door to the reception room and looked at him impassively. "First shoot is in Glendale. A stripper who teaches lap dancing to housewives at lunch."

"That's pathetic."

"Give it a chance. This isn't your kind of documentary, Stef. It's mine."

"Your kind would change topics every five minutes."

Sabrina's gaze chilled. "Leave your card with Laeticia. I'll e-mail you the details. And Stef?" She paused. "Don't think you know me just because I made the mistake of sleeping with you a long time ago."

4

"SO WHAT DO YOU THINK, the green or the cream?" Kelly asked, nibbling on her thumb as she stared at the couches arrayed across the showroom at Civilization.

Sabrina sat on the cream couch experimentally, running her hand over the woven cotton fabric. "You know me, I'd probably go for the leopard one. You should ask Paige. Or better yet, get her to take you to the Pacific Design Center."

"Oh yeah, sure." Kelly dropped down beside her. "Paige would blow my budget on a single coffee table, then tell me the way to decorate was to invest in one signature piece at a time. And five years later, I'd actually have a completed living room."

Sabrina fought a smile. "Well, it's not going to be perfect overnight."

"I don't want perfect. I just want a room that's not furnished in Early American Garage Sale. You know Cilla offered to let me pick what I wanted from the Danforth home shop at cost," she asked with a grin.

"Why didn't you take her up on it?"

"Uh, right. Like I could even afford that at cost."

Sabrina turned and looked across the room at the

array of couches. "What color are you doing the walls in again?"

"Sage." Kelly handed over the paint chip. "Cream trim. The coffee table's blond wood."

Sabrina rose and began stalking between the couches, glancing at the chip in her hand.

Kelly trailed her anxiously. "Just don't do a Paige on me. Nothing in the back three rows."

"I should get myself some furniture one of these days," Sabrina muttered.

"Why don't you? What I don't understand is why you live in Venice when you could live anywhere."

Sabrina shrugged and leaned over to inspect the fabric of a floral couch. "What's wrong with Venice?"

"Why not Brentwood? Or the Westwood Corridor?"

"It's not like it's a wreck. I like Venice. I like the canals. It feels right to me."

"But you've got all of L.A. at your fingertips," Kelly protested.

"I suppose," Sabrina said absently. "But I'm happy where I am."

"I wish I could say that."

"But you've got a great little flat," Sabrina protested, thinking of Kelly's little 1940s courtyard apartment.

"Sure, if you don't count the triple-X movie theater on the main boulevard."

"At least you've got entertainment nearby."

"Sorry, I'll take my porn at home like everyone else, thanks. Anyway, it's not the flat. I just wish the neighborhood were better. Next promotion, I'm moving." She smiled faintly.

"What about a roommate?"

Kelly shook her head again, more definitely. "No way. I like living alone. I mean, it was one thing to share a house with all you guys when we were in college, but it's different now. I like my privacy."

"Are you sure? You could move in with me."

Kelly nodded. "Naw, I like being able to come home and have wild sex on the kitchen counter if I feel like it. But if you move to Brentwood sometime, you can ask me again."

"Okay." Sabrina slowed, then walked purposefully to a couch set up next to a distressed armoire. "That one."

It was an overstuffed sofa in a deep plum, with a slight deco flare to the arms.

"You're out of your mind. It's a green room. Why would I want to go with purple?"

"It'll look ravishing, trust me." Sabrina's tone was brisk. "Green is too matchy matchy, cream is boring, slate is predictable. This will be just the bit of shock that you need."

Kelly frowned. "This isn't one of your bizarre design statements, is it? I don't want bohemian chic, I want something that looks stylish."

"Trust me," Sabrina said simply and held out the paint chip.

"Okay, a glass of the ten-year tawny and one cosmopolitan," said the waitress. "I'll be right back with your cheese plate."

They sat at a patio table at Morels in the Grove, watching people walk by. A cross between Disney's Main

Street USA and the Mall of America, spiced with a snip of Paris, the Grove had sprung up next to the L.A. Farmers' Market and had quickly become a place to be. Kids loved it for the old-fashioned streetcar that ran down pavement untouched by a car. Parents liked it because it was safe and contained, and full of goodies to buy.

Sabrina liked it because it held Morels, the only restaurant in town that boasted a cheese list as long as its wine list.

Sabrina raised her glass of port. "To your new furniture."

"To you, for helping me choose," Kelly countered, clicking her glass against Sabrina's.

"The living room's going to look great."

"I'm actually excited about the kitchen table. I'm just trying not to think about the fact that I just killed my savings account. How in the hell do people make themselves buy houses," she muttered, taking a sip of her drink.

"Oh, come on, remember your promotion. You should be rolling in it now."

"I don't know about that, although certainly senior writers make better money than associate editors."

"There, see? How's the new job going, anyway?"

Kelly grinned. "Pretty well. I've been getting out on interviews a lot. I just got to report from the set of Matt Ramsay's new film," she said with a gleam in her eye. "Hey, how come you never invite him to any of our parties, anyway? You never even invited him to the drama productions back when we were all at UCLA."

"Trust me, you don't want to get anywhere near my cousin."

"What, is he a jerk? You've always talked about him like he's a nice guy."

"Oh, the nicest. Totally sincere. Fatally." Their waiter set their cheese plate at the table. Sabrina shook her head and reached out to spread Gorgonzola on a slice of brioche. "That's the problem, he's fatally sincere. A woman catches his eye and suddenly he's nuts for her. He's telling everyone who'll listen that she's the one. And the woman, whoever she is, eventually falls for it, because he believes it himself. Then he sees that she's only human and the infatuation wears off. After that, it just gets ugly. He's an incredibly creative and interesting guy in every other way, but I'd never in a million years let anyone I actually liked date him."

"Sabrina, how long have you known me?"

Sabrina counted in her head. "Nine years. God, has it really been that long?"

"Probably. And in all that time, have I ever said anything about looking for true love?"

"No, but—"

"Have I?"

"No."

"Then what makes you think I'd go all doe-eyed over your cousin?"

"It's this mind control thing he gets going. You wouldn't mean to, but you wouldn't be able to help it."

"Trust me, I'd help it." Kelly waved the waiter over and ordered another drink. "Anyway, never mind. I'm not interested in any guy who's going to go all gaga over me anyway. I want a good time, good sex and a hot career. I'd rather stick with the ones who know how the game's played." She waved her hand. "Speaking of games, how's the great American documentary going?"

"Okay," Sabrina said noncommittally, nibbling on an almond. "So are you going to the premiere?"

"Don't try to change the subject. Last time I saw you, you were dancing on air over this thing. What, are you having problems now?"

"No, everything's fine, great."

Kelly's eyes narrowed fractionally; then she relaxed, glancing over at the dancing water fountain next to the restaurant. "You know, we have known each other a long time," she said, leaning back in her chair and looking at Sabrina. "I don't think I've ever told you, but did you know that every time you lie, there's this little muscle by the corner of your eye that starts to twitch?"

Sabrina choked on her drink.

"What's going on, Pantolini? Something's up."

"Nothing's up."

"Boy, look at that thing go," Kelly said with enjoyment, and began digging in her purse. "I know I've got a mirror in here somewhere. You oughtta take a look. It's really something."

Sabrina scowled at her. "I get the idea."

"So?"

"I just had some problems lining up a director. Mine bolted for another project before we had him locked in."

"Are you going to be able to find someone else in time?"

Sabrina chewed on her lip. "That's where the problem comes in. My uncle Gus came up with someone, which was a good thing since I'd scoured the town and couldn't find anybody."

"Why do I want to say uh-oh?"

"It's Stef Costas."

Kelly blinked at her. "Stef?"

"Stef."

"The Greek god? Are you out of your *mind?*"

"It's okay, Kelly."

"Rina, there has to be someone else around. You can't work with this guy. You talk about not letting your friends go near your cousin with a ten-foot pole, what about this?"

"It's history, Kelly, eight years ago. It's nothing I can't handle," Sabrina muttered.

"Are you sure of that? Don't forget what he put you through. I haven't. I was the shoulder you cried on."

And Sabrina would never stop being grateful for it. "I was nineteen then. I've gotten smarter. I can work with the guy without letting old news get in the way."

Kelly gave her a level look. "I hope you're right."

"It's business, that's all. If I've learned nothing else since working for Uncle Gus it's that you get the job done, no matter what." Sabrina's voice was shaded with intensity. "You don't let anything get in the way of the job, especially nothing personal."

"Nothing personal? He broke your heart."

"Look," Sabrina's voice softened. "I appreciate your being concerned, but it's okay, really. We set some ground rules. He knows I'm in charge."

"You sure about that? Because it would be a really bad idea to be going into this thinking that you're going to rewrite history or something. Sexual politics never got anyone anywhere."

"Trust me, the only thing I'm thinking about is getting this pilot done the best way I know how. As far as I'm concerned, Stef Costas is just another person on the set."

Kelly shook her head. "Sure. And denial is a river in Egypt."

5

"SO WHAT GOT YOU interested in teaching lap dancing?" Sabrina sat on a couch next to a ripe redhead named Cherry Devine, ignoring the lights and the microphone dangling overhead. "I mean, if you teach wives and girlfriends to do this for their significant others, isn't that ultimately going to cut into your clientele?"

The lush stripper threw her head back and laughed. "Honey, the guys who come to see me are looking for a pro, not someone they really have to deal with." Her red silk robe gaped open with a studied carelessness to display the lingerie—and the soft skin—beneath. The camera angle worked, Sabrina decided, giving a nod to Stef. It made Cherry the sole focus, so that they could edit down to just comments rather than Q and A in postproduction.

Stef gave a quick hand signal to the cameraman to zoom in just slightly. Black-eyed and intense, his dark hair curling onto the collar of his denim shirt, Stef looked calm and in command. He also looked outrageously sexy, Sabrina thought. Which was something she had to stop noticing, and pronto.

"How did you wind up in lap dancing?"

Cherry dangled a cigarette from her fingers with innate theatricality. "I like showing off my body. Being a stripper is one way to make a living at it."

"It doesn't bother you to be on stage naked with a room full of men watching you?" The question wasn't part of the script, but Sabrina followed her instincts.

Cherry's laugh was husky and confident. "When I'm up on that stage, I own the room. Every man with a pulse wants me. I'm the one in control." She blew a stream of smoke toward the ceiling and glanced appraisingly at Stef. "Being able to get a man hot is the most powerful feeling in the world."

"So teach us how it's done," Sabrina suggested, resisting the sudden urge to grind her teeth.

Cherry stood and eased her robe off one shoulder. "It'll be my pleasure."

The red and gold living room was crowded with the six couples who'd come for her class, as well as the film crew. "Okay, each couple, pull up a chair. Guys, take a seat. Ladies, stand nearby," she said, setting a straight-backed chair in the center of the living room to demonstrate.

Sabrina moved over by Stef. "Aren't you going to move in with the handheld to get footage on some of these people?" She kept her voice low.

"In good time."

"How much time do you think we have?" she asked.

"Look, if we move around too much now, we're going to draw their attention. Right now, we stay in one place, they'll start relaxing and you can get some good candid footage. Just calm down and let me direct, all right?"

Sabrina stared at him a moment, then subsided, turning her attention back to Cherry.

"My usual assistant isn't here," Cherry said, "which means I don't have anyone to demonstrate on. I could use a spare red-blooded male." She rested a hand on the chair back and glanced around the room; then her eyes brightened. "You, big boy," she crooked her finger at Stef, who stood next to his cameraman, Kev. "Have a seat."

"Sorry, I'm busy," he said tersely.

"Ooh, I just love masterful men," she cooed, walking up to him to curl her fingers into his shirtfront. "Just give me a few minutes of your time. You don't even have to do anything but sit." She turned, still holding on to his shirt and started to tug him across the room.

Emotions chased through Sabrina in rapid succession—confusion, shock, dismay, and a surprising spurt of jealousy. "He can't do it," she bit out. "Pick someone else."

Cherry looked back curiously at Sabrina. Her eyes flickered to Stef and then her gaze sharpened. "Ah." Slowly, the corners of Cherry's mouth drew up into a smile.

"He can't appear in the footage. He's the director," Sabrina persisted.

Cherry gave her a glance. "Don't worry, sugar pie, I'll make sure I stay between him and the camera."

With a glance to make sure Stef was seated, she sashayed over to punch the Play button on the CD player. Rock music filled the room, not the slow bluesy number Sabrina had expected, but something a little faster, with a beat that thudded into her brain. There was something familiar about that beat, she thought. Not too fast, not too slow, it had the beat of…

It had the beat of sex.

Cherry turned back to her class. "You've got to have music you can move to. There is no right or wrong, so long as it's sexy to you and your partner, it works." Around the room, here and there, people nodded to the beat. One of the men, who looked like a junior high school principal, reached up and ran a hand down his partner's hip; she leaned back against him with a smile of promise.

"Thanks, Paul, you just handed me the perfect lead-in," Cherry said to him. "I'm sure you all know the basic idea of a lap dance—the dancer is allowed to touch the client, but he's not allowed to touch her. Or him," she added looking around at the men in the room. "Don't think that your job is just to sit there, fellas. We'll have you doing the dances by the end of the lesson." There was a bit of uncomfortable laughter. "By holding back, by not allowing the client to touch you, you turn touching you into the only thing he can think about. That's where the tease comes in."

Suddenly, she began to move to the beat, the sway of hip and flow of shoulders all the more riveting for the lack of introduction. She shrugged her shoulders and the robe slipped down her arms to a crimson pool at her feet. "The tease and the promise are everything." She ran a hand through Stef's hair as she straddled his lap. "Of course, everyone in the room here is lucky—you'll actually get your dancer to come through on that promise, won't you," she said, looking into Stef's taut face.

Sabrina could cheerfully have scratched the woman's eyes out. It shouldn't bother her, she told herself, watching Cherry slide around on Stef while a roomful of people eyed them avidly. It didn't matter to her what he did. She was over him.

She had to be.

Eventually, Cherry finished and Sabrina's jaw loosened. The stripper threw Sabrina a grin and then addressed her class. "All right, ladies, listen to the music. Now just stand in front of your man and touch yourself. Run your hands down your hips, up your arms, or anywhere else you'd like to," she said, demonstrating. "Get yourself turned on and get him thinking about touching you—because he can't, and you want him to want it more than he's ever wanted anything. You want to blow the top of his head off."

Sabrina looked around the room as Stef rose to return to directing.

"Did you have fun?" she asked, just a bit of bite in her voice.

"Did I have a choice?" he returned. "You're running this shoot, why didn't you pull her off?"

"Weren't you the one who always said you never did anything you didn't choose to?"

"You want to last in this business, you learn to cooperate."

A woman could drown in those black eyes, she thought. But not her. "Great. Then how about if you start by getting some footage with a handheld?"

"Not now."

"Oh, really. If not now, when?"

"When they stop looking around at one another. You go with how it feels." He shrugged. "Maybe in a little while. Maybe never."

"Thanks for being so precise."

"Maybe when you stop drawing attention to us by talking."

"It's not like they don't know we're here," Kev murmured from behind Stef. "Let's see if we can blend in. Sabrina, maybe if you move around the room and let them start talking to you, it'll get things going."

With his jeans, T-shirt and untidily cropped hair, Kev looked like someone's kid brother, but there was a casual efficiency to his motions that spoke of long experience. He might have a point, Sabrina acknowledged. She wondered if it said something about her character that it was easier to take suggestions from him than from Stef.

She began to wander slowly through the room, watching the students. It was just like life. Some of the couples were earnest and focused on doing the exercise properly, as though they were going to be graded. Some were self-conscious, looking miserably aware of being in public and on camera. Most of them, though, looked like they were just getting turned on—not just by the lesson, but by watching their fellow students.

So maybe the tidy Glendale neighborhoods weren't just about coffee klatches and the PTA, she thought with a smile. Maybe they had their share of swingers, too. She'd intended this segment as a tool to draw the average viewer into a world where sexual rules went out the window. Each segment of the doc would take them further, bit by bit, so they wouldn't really notice it. But maybe she'd miscalculated. Maybe, just maybe, Middle America had come further than she realized.

"What a cool thing," she murmured, starting when she realized that she'd spoken aloud.

"We just wanted to spice things up a little bit," said a thin brunette named Miranda, casually flipping her silk robe to cover her bare breast. "You've got to be open to new things."

Miranda's partner George, who looked like he might work at the local lube shop, just nodded. Sabrina suspected he'd be all in favor of anything leading to quality sheet time.

"We tried a tantric sex class, but I wanted something with more action," Miranda said. "Of course, sitting in the middle of a roomful of people having sex isn't so bad," she giggled, and began to move on George's lap again.

Sabrina moved over to the school principal and his partner. He was stripped down to a silk G-string and giving his partner a surprisingly good lap dance. He rubbed his green silk-clad crotch against the blonde, letting her feel his hard-on while he traced his fingers down over her breasts. "Yeah, you like that, don't you," he whispered, staring into her eyes.

Now this was a motivated man, Sabrina thought. This was a group of people who knew how to make it fun, how to make it sexy, how to make it about them.

Cherry crossed over to where Sabrina stood with Kev and Stef. "So, are you enjoying yourselves?"

"It's been educational," Sabrina said. "You always get a crowd like this?"

"Sometimes more. You should come out on a weekend night. People really let their hair down then," she said with a sidelong glance at Stef. "I think you'd like it."

"Well, it looks like we've got everything we need," Sabrina said thinly.

Cherry glanced from Stef to Sabrina and nodded. "Excellent." The song ended and she raised her voice a little. "Of course, it hardly seems fair to send off the film crew without a little bit of instruction, does it, gang?" she asked the group. "You two," she crooked her finger at Sabrina and Stef, "over here."

Surprise had Sabrina laughing. Some other time with some other person, maybe, but Stef? No way. "Thanks, but we need to finish up here and get going."

"Nope, you've got to do at least one dance if you're going to report on it. Them's the rules."

Sabrina picked up her notepad. "I learned plenty by watching."

"Well, then it will be easy to demonstrate for us."

Suddenly, it wasn't nearly as amusing. "I'm hardly dressed for it," she said, gesturing down at her miniskirt.

"We're not exactly dressed ourselves," Cherry purred. "Besides, short skirts work well for lap dancing."

Stef shook his head. "I've done my volunteer work today."

Kev suddenly became intensely interested in reviewing some playback, eyes locked on his equipment.

Cherry studied Stef coolly. "You know, that's an awfully uptight attitude to take, especially since everyone in this room has signed a release to let you film us for national broadcast without asking for a dime." She looked around at the women standing in lingerie and the men, many of whom were wearing only robes. There were murmurs and nods of agreements, then someone began a slow, measured clap.

Cherry clearly liked calling the shots and putting them on the spot seemed to amuse her. "I think it's a gesture of good faith for you to at least run through a minute or two of a dance," she insisted. The clapping grew louder, augmented by whistles.

Sabrina leaned over to Stef. "Got any ideas, Mr. Red-blooded Male?"

"You're the one who got us into this. You get us out."

"I'm not sure I can," she confessed.

Stef gave her a long look and raked his hair back out of his eyes. He turned to Kev. "I'm not expecting to hear about this again."

"What? Sorry, I wasn't paying attention. Too busy," Kev assured him, eye still pressed to the viewfinder. A corner of his mouth tugged up.

"Make it fast," Stef muttered to Sabrina, then strode over to sit in the straight-back chair. It would be okay, Sabrina told herself as she followed. She'd just pretend it was someone besides Stef. Who knew, maybe it would even be fun.

Cherry gave them a glance over her shoulder and put a new CD into the player. Something about the smirk that flickered over her mouth looked entirely too satisfied, Sabrina thought. Then the music started. It flowed out of the speakers, a sexy, bluesy number with a powerful beat. Cherry turned up the volume a bit, then turned it up some more.

Sabrina took a deep breath and put her hands on Stef's shoulders. In clothing, he looked deceptively lanky, so the solid mass of muscle under her fingers came as a surprise. He'd matured since they'd been lovers. Then, he'd been little more than a boy. Now, he was a man, and she could feel it in every fiber of him.

She stepped in and lowered herself to barely brush his legs.

"No perching on his knees," Cherry instructed. "Get in there. I want to see contact."

Sabrina rested her full weight on him and slid in a fraction closer. Stef looked at her with the same unruffled stare he'd given her in her office. Sudden annoyance surged through her. He'd managed to kiss her and throw her for a loop without losing an ounce of calm. Not this time. This time she'd pull a reaction from him. Oh yes, this time she'd definitely be the one in control.

She settled her hands more solidly on his shoulders and moved forward until the satin of her thong was firmly against his crotch, her silky short skirt sliding back to expose tanned legs. Someone whooped, and Sabrina grinned despite herself. Around them, people swayed to the music as though they were in a strip club, watching the show.

"Now move, honey," Cherry said in her ear. "Make him sweat." Sabrina nodded to the beat and then, as she caught the rhythm, began working herself back and forth on Stef's lap. The twill of his khakis felt smooth against the backs of her thighs. His zipper pressed at her mons, then lower. The thrill of arousal took her by surprise. It told her that she was wetter than she realized. When she pressed again, the slick friction made her catch her breath.

"You're the dancer," Cherry said. "You're allowed to touch him."

Focus, Sabrina told herself, concentrating on wiping that expressionless look off his face. With a slow, teasing smile, she trailed the back of her fingers up the side of his cheek and into his hair. He'd be hard-pressed to avoid looking down her tank top at her breasts, she realized, leaning closer. She took a deep breath, knowing that it made them stand out more, and leaned in to nuzzle his forehead.

"You can stop this any time you want," Stef said, his voice tight.

"Why? Am I making you uncomfortable?" she whispered, wiggling against his crotch, in part to infuriate him and maybe in part because it felt so damned good.

A muscle jumped in his jaw. His black eyes bored into hers. "What do you think?"

Then she felt a sudden pressure against her, a hard fullness where there'd been none before. Sabrina ran a fingertip teasingly into the collar of his shirt and leaned in against him. "Is it turning you on, is that why you want to stop?" The surge of lust that rocketed through her made her dizzy. He was rock-hard against her now. If she hadn't been so close to him, she might have missed his soft groan. Sabrina leaned back in surprise.

She'd wanted a reaction from him. What she felt now wasn't triumph, though, but raw, naked desire. She wanted to tear his clothes off, have him take her then and there, bent over the couch, down on the floor—

"Someone get a bucket of cold water for these two," Cherry called gleefully.

Sabrina blinked in surprise. For just that moment,

she'd forgotten they were in a roomful of people. She'd been totally focused on what was happening between her and Stef. Getting immersed in him was a dangerous thing to let happen.

She'd learned that the hard way.

Sabrina stood up slowly, to give Stef the benefit of time to calm down. Amid the noise and motion in the room, his own appearance went unnoticed.

It was nothing, she told herself as she straightened her skirt and turned mechanically to pack up her notes and files. It would have happened with any good-looking guy she was rubbing around on like that. It didn't mean anything. She and Stef were through with a capital *T*.

She just needed to remember to keep it that way.

Gradually, as the room emptied, she started to find the humor in what had happened.

Cherry walked them to the door. Sabrina turned to her before stepping outside. "We'll send you information on the test screening. We'd love to have you come."

"I've been on screen before, but not like that." The redhead smiled broadly. "It might be fun…I hope you found here what you were looking for."

"It was, ah, educational," Sabrina responded.

"I'll bet," Cherry said, and her gaze flicked toward Stef. "I'd tell you to come on back any time for advanced lessons, but I think you've got the technique down just fine. Good luck."

Baffled, Sabrina shook hands with her. "And to you."

"I SEE YOU HAVEN'T CHANGED," Stef said tightly as they walked toward the filming truck where the crew was already loading up equipment. He wasn't sure who he was more angry at—Sabrina for the lap dance or himself for the fact that his system still hadn't leveled out. Get her out of his head. Yeah, right. Smart thinking. "This is just the kind of thing you used to pull back at UCLA and it's exactly why I didn't want to work with you to begin with. You're a loose cannon."

Sabrina just laughed. "Oh, lighten up, already. She wanted to yank our chains and she did. So what? You know we got great footage out of this."

"It wasn't about the footage and you know it. You were completely out of line." And she'd sucked him right in.

"Your problem is that you've always taken yourself too seriously," she said, unclipping her purse. "The brilliant, visionary Stef Costas. Well, that's not who you are on this one. You're anonymous, so why don't you relax and enjoy it?" She turned to walk toward her car.

Stef's eyes narrowed and he took two quick steps, turning her and dragging her into his arms. He saw her look of shock for an instant. Then his mouth closed on hers and vision was irrelevant.

It was more than a kiss. It was all the frustration and arousal of the past few hours, pouring from him into her. He knew she thought she had him under control, but she was wrong. He wanted to devour her, to show her who was master, to lead them both into a blind, clawing frenzy.

He'd watched her during the filming, moving through the room in her tank top, her skirt swishing against those fabulous legs. Then sitting there motionless during her lap dance, unable to react, staring as her mocking smile turned into the flush of arousal. And remembering what it was like to drive himself deep into her, knowing what it was like to have those legs twined around him.

Knowing how she cried out when she came.

As he felt Sabrina begin to match him for fire and flash, he fought to drag himself back from the brink that she pulled him toward. He had to get a grip, Stef realized dimly, struggling for control. If they were going to go there, he'd be the one to lead.

The rest of the crew was around somewhere, maybe even watching them. Somehow, he couldn't make it matter.

Trying to manage his breathing, he released her and stepped back. "No more little stunts like that again."

Sabrina's stunned expression gradually cleared. "Is that what you think this was about?" she asked incredulously. "You can't handle the fact that you wanted me? You've got hormones like everybody else, Stef. Learn to deal with them." She pulled her keys out of her purse. "We always were good in bed. It was everywhere else that needed work."

6

STEF LEANED BACK in his chair and stared up at the bare
pipes and girders that ran across the ceiling of his office. So maybe a warehouse in the commercial area in
Culver City wasn't exactly a high-rent address, but it
provided enough space for the right price, not to mention skylights and parking. He swiveled his chair to
look out into the reception area, where vivid abstract
paintings from several up-and-coming artists studded
the industrial white walls. Okay, so practical only went
so far. Even he needed to recharge his visual batteries
occasionally.

Kev sprawled on the black leather couch at the other
end of the room. Stef had meant it when he'd told Sabrina that he didn't work without Kev. More precisely,
he didn't work effectively without him. Maybe it was
seven years of back-to-back shooting, but they managed
to communicate without words. Sometimes Kev knew
what Stef wanted almost before he'd decided it. Snappy
work for a young guy with a soul patch-Fu Manchu
combo and a dubiously laundered T-shirt. The fact that
he was a brilliant cinematographer only showed up
when you saw him work. Kev's untidy crop and slacker

style didn't inspire much confidence from producers. His camerawork did.

"So, I always wondered what it would be like to work with one of those big-time Hollywood people," Kev said idly, tossing a Hacky Sack in the air above him and catching it rhythmically. "Besides you, of course," he added.

"Besides me," Stef said dryly.

"Sabrina Pantolini, of the famous Pantolinis."

"Can we talk about something else, please? Like lighting?" Stef made notes on a lined pad in front of him. "I don't want to be hauling a million reflectors and flags out to the location if we're not going to use them, and I don't want to light it like a porn set."

"Oh, I don't know, irony's very hip these days."

"Kev." Stef's voice held an unmistakable note of warning.

"Tell me what you want, chief, you'll get it," Kev said, and returned to tossing the ball. "Although judging by her looks, I bet our producer would be all for it. So is it true what they say about sleeping your way to the top in this town?"

Stef's head snapped around. After a minute he turned back to his notepad. "Not in your case. So are we going to talk lighting or are you just here to bug me?"

"You know me, always ready for work," Kev said agreeably. "Whatever it takes to move the project ahead. I'll even volunteer for extra duty, like working off some of our producer's excess tension, say."

This time, Stef turned even faster. "If you're not in the mood to work, maybe you ought to leave," he suggested.

"Touchy." Kev sounded amused, not chastened. "But still, not just one but two lap dances. You need someone to take the heat off you. You know me, I'll do my part for the team."

"Believe me, it wasn't as hot as it looked."

Kev laughed at Stef's glower. "Yeah, you looked like you were having a terrible time."

"Fine. Next time, I'll take the camera and let you deal with it."

"Unless you want to share…"

This time, Stef snapped his pen down. "What's your point, Kev?"

"No point." He returned to tossing the ball.

Stef started to turn back to his desk. "So do you think—"

"Looks like you guys go back a ways."

"College. What's it to you?"

"You're seeming a little edgy, bud."

"If I'm edgy, it's because you're ticking me off. Why are you on me about Sabrina?" Bad enough that images of her kept intruding in his thoughts. He didn't need a reminder that he'd lost control on the job the day before.

"Hey, I'm just trying to figure out the lay of the land here. I mean, I'm trying to do my usual world-class job and if you two are going to be having lovers' quarrels—"

"Put a lid on it. Any old business I have with Sabrina is not going to get in the way of the shoot."

Kev barely suppressed a smirk. "It does when you're making out in front of the cargo van I'm trying to load. I mean, don't get me wrong, she's a step up from your usual type. Guess you had better taste back in college."

"Look, don't—"

The phone rang, the electronic burble loud in the room.

"Costas."

"Stef, it's Sabrina."

It's Sabrina. There had been a time when those words would have stopped him dead. Now, he let his breath out slowly. "Right. What do you need?" Professionals. They both needed to concentrate on being professionals.

"I'm making arrangements for the New York shoot. Are you going to ship the camera equipment ahead or take it on the plane with you?"

"Take it with. I don't like to let that kind of equipment out of my hands. By the way, we should talk about those street interviews you want to bridge segments with. We should stay an extra day or two and knock them off in Manhattan. New York's perfect for them."

"I've already cleared it to shoot in Santa Monica on the Promenade and in Hollywood on Melrose."

It was news to him. "New York is going to give you a better vibe." He picked up the pen and began making a pattern of tight, sharp hatch marks. "Think about it, we can use Times Square, Greenwich Village. Great stuff."

"It's not possible, especially at this point." Her brisk tone brooked no opposition.

"As director, I get some input here. It's not hard to pull a permit in New York."

"Have you ever shot there?" Her voice was curt.

Stef noticed Kev's interested look and struggled not to react. "No, why?"

"A permit's the least of our problems. It's a union town, Stef, remember?"

"So?"

"So stick to directing and leave me to do my job." There was a click in his ear and the line buzzed.

He cursed and reached for her business card.

"Nice to see that you and our producer continue to see eye to eye." Kev started tossing the ball again.

Stef ignored him, stabbing at the keypad of the phone. They had to get a handle on this or they were never going to get anything done, he thought, listening to the tones that signified ringing across town.

"This is Sabrina."

"Don't ever hang up on me again while we're working together." He bit off the words.

"Oh, I'm sorry about that," she said insincerely. "I said goodbye while I was putting the receiver down. You must not have heard."

"You keep telling me you're a professional, Sabrina. Act like it."

He heard the quick intake of her breath and a second or two went by. Her self-control had improved, that much was clear. There'd been a time when a provocation like that would have produced an angry torrent of invective. Now, it seemed, she thought first.

"All right, let's start again."

"If we're going to work together, I'd say it's critical." He meant it to stop her and it did.

"Let bygones be bygones?" she asked finally. "You, of all people, should know it's not that easy."

"No," he agreed. "That doesn't mean we shouldn't set it aside while we're working, though. Nothing we say is going to change our history, but we've got a project to finish here." The seconds ticked by while he focused on the electronic silence in his ear.

"You're right," she said grudgingly. He could only imagine what it cost her.

"Good. Now you can explain to me why you don't want to shoot street interviews in New York."

"Like I said, it's a union town. That means the cost jumps for everything from moving a light two feet down the street to stringing electrical cable." The certainty was still there, but the defiance was muted. "If we show up with a non-union shoot, they'll be on us like flies, heckling, interrupting the shoot, sabotaging. They'll be trying to unionize the crew. Meanwhile, we'll have to pay for police and fire coverage, street closure, and everything else you can think of."

"For a two-hour evening shoot?"

"A street shoot, Stef. I've been a production manager for five years. Give me credit for knowing something, okay?"

Now it was his turn to pause. If he were to stick to their agreement, he needed to respect her decisions as producer. That didn't mean he had to like them, but there had been plenty of other producers he'd disagreed with in the past. It went with the territory. "All right. You say L.A., we do L.A."

"What?" Her flummoxed tone made him smile for the first time. "Could you repeat that?"

"We shoot where you want to shoot."

"Well." She regrouped quickly. "As long as you're feeling accommodating, maybe we can cover a few more points."

He shook his head. "Not so fast. Let's close on this decision and take it step by step from now on."

"Okay," she said slowly. "I guess you've got a deal."

SABRINA HUNG UP the phone in bemusement. She wasn't sure whom she'd been talking to, but it wasn't the Stef she knew. Unless she was very much mistaken, he'd just extended an olive branch. She didn't know what surprised her more—that he'd done it or that she'd accepted.

The phone rang. Stef, calling to change his mind, she thought immediately, and scooped the receiver up. "You said it, I heard it. No fair changing your mind."

"But I didn't think it through," a female voice protested.

Sabrina laughed and relaxed. "Hi, Kelly."

"So who did you think it was going to be?"

"Oh, Stef and I were just having another preproduction chat."

"Always a fun time."

"Actually, he was pretty reasonable."

"Now I'm scared."

Sabrina dug in her desk drawer for some lip balm. "Don't be."

"Maybe we should go out for lunch and talk about this."

Sabrina thought longingly of a salad in an outdoor café on Melrose and sighed. "I've got too much to do here. Give me a rain check?"

"You were a lot more fun in the old days."

"I'm fun now. I'm more fun than a barrel full of monkeys, more fun than an E-ticket ride." Sabrina ran the balm over her lips.

"You're behind the times," Kelly told her. "They don't even have E-ticket rides any more."

"That's what's wrong with the modern world. Everything's all-inclusive, all you can eat. There's nothing you have to work for any more."

"Sure there is. I have to work for a paycheck. You have to work to get your doc done, and with the Greek god, it'll definitely qualify as work."

"Believe me," Sabrina sighed, "I'd like nothing better than to have another director, but I've got to get this baby made."

"Yeah, yeah."

Sabrina hesitated. "I need to show myself that I can do this, Kelly," she said slowly. "And that I can do it with Stef around, because if I can get through it with him, I can pretty much get through it with anyone."

"And there's not one little part of you that's wondering what it would be like to get back in his pants for a day?"

"No." Sabrina had a sudden, vivid flash of the feel of Stef kissing her, the promise and the taunt. "No," she said more positively.

Kelly snorted. "I'll remind you of that later on. Anyway, I'm going to give you some good news for a change. How'd you like to get some nice, free publicity?"

"Nothing's free. What's the catch?" Sabrina listened to the suppressed excitement in Kelly's voice.

"No catch." She cleared her throat. "At least not much of one. My editor at *Hot Ticket* has been saying for the last two years that we don't do enough on docs. He says Hollywood pays 'em lip service, but it's never serious about them."

Sabrina's grin was wry. "Tell me about it."

"Well, I need a project to wow him with. I mean, I just got the promotion. I want to show him he was right about me. So I pitched him a story on your documentary and he bit. I've got a travel budget, time off to spend on set, the works," she finished triumphantly. "Depending on how well he likes it, it could even be a series."

"You wouldn't have any ulterior motive in all of this, would you?" Sabrina asked dryly.

"Besides world domination in entertainment reporting?"

"Oh, I was thinking more like trying to be my chaperone, your being so sure that I'm going to do something I regret."

"Trying to keep an eye on you and that director formerly known as boyfriend from hell that you've decided to work with? Hey, you want to make yourself crazy, what business is it of mine?"

"I'm sure you'll tell me soon enough." Sabrina heard the clacking of computer keys. Kelly, an inveterate multitasker, was no doubt responding to e-mail while they talked.

There was a flurry of typing and an especially loud clack. "Look, all I want is the inside scoop for a great article. A few interviews with your crew, a few shots of your precious director at work."

Sabrina could just imagine how Stef would react to the news. Now that she thought about it, the idea didn't seem so bad. "We can certainly use the publicity." It was a no-brainer, she reasoned. Every project needed exposure, especially documentaries. Opening the set to a reporter could increase the buzz for her project. Just because Kelly was a friend was no guarantee it would be a totally positive article, but at least they wouldn't get savaged completely. Who knew, maybe she'd even have an easier time getting funding the next time around, rather than paying for most things out of her own pocket.

And if she enjoyed the prospect of Stef's discomfiture, that didn't mean she was breaking their truce, did it?

7

SABRINA TURNED OFF the central California highway into a single-lane road, her wheels chattering over the cattle guard that spanned the opening in the white-painted fence. There was no sign, only a mailbox topped with a carved wooden knight on horseback. The dirt road wound over a bleached gold hillside dotted with live oaks and then curved behind a stand of eucalyptus. The pungent scent of mesquite streamed in through her open window.

"We made pretty good time," Kelly said. With her tousled blond hair and her faded shorts, she looked more like a surfer chick than a reporter.

"We were supposed to be here ten minutes ago," Sabrina reminded her. "The crew's going to be waiting."

"It's a two-hour drive up from L.A. Being ten minutes late is not a crisis. I mean, it's not like they fire off a starting gun when they open their little fair doohickey, do they?"

"You'd be surprised what they do. Anyway, we've got a lot to cover and only one day to do it in."

"How much is there to see? People in costume, getting sexy."

"I see you didn't do your research."

"My research is you and your film crew, not what you're filming," Kelly said carelessly, then stopped. "So what exactly are you filming?"

Sabrina grinned at her as they topped a rise. "Take a look."

For an instant, it felt as though the truck had become a time machine, whisking them back to Elizabethan England. White-daubed, thatched-roof cottages clustered around a grassy square dotted with market stalls. Small figures that looked like peasants lined up at the tables of an outdoor tavern. Behind lay a Tudor-style manor house, with crimson-and-white banners streaming from its towers. A wooden palisade surrounded the whole area.

Kelly stared. "What are they, Renaissance fair fanatics? Who on earth would build something like this all the way out here?"

Sabrina shrugged, following the path downward to the parking area. "An eccentric billionaire with a lot of friends."

The production van, she saw, was already in the parking area, which meant that Laeticia and the crew had made it. The plain white cargo van would be full of lighting equipment for the gaffer to use, not to mention sound gear and cameras.

She pulled between the van and an olive-drab Jeep. Stef's, she was betting. It was like him: practical, not flashy, but tough and capable. She stepped out onto the packed dirt of the parking area. The first order of business was to get the shoot rolling.

"Morning." Stef materialized from behind the Jeep.

How was it that he took her breath away even after all this time, she wondered. The light breeze caught the hair that curved down onto his forehead and pulled at the shirttails of the faded madras shirt he wore. The morning sun only brought out the gold in his skin. Nothing could mask the intensity in his dark eyes.

"Good morning. Have a good drive up?" She slung her satchel over her shoulder and shoved her keys into the pocket of her cargo pants.

"Yeah, actually. I took Pacific Coast Highway through Malibu."

It surprised her that he'd chosen the narrow road that wound between the Pacific and the rugged coastal bluffs instead of the more direct inland freeways. More of the new Stef? "Well you had perfect weather for it. You remember Kelly, don't you?"

"Of course." He nodded and shook Kelly's hand.

"Kelly's an editor at *Hot Ticket* now. She's doing a feature on the making of the documentary."

"I'm just going to hang around and watch the filming today, but I'll want to interview you later," Kelly put in.

Sabrina braced herself for the explosion. Surely he'd go into a rant about his sterling reputation and how he didn't want anyone to know he was working on her sex documentary. But outside of the subtle setting of his jaw—darkened with the previous day's beard—he didn't react. She relaxed fractionally.

"We move the equipment first," he said, nodding at Kev, who had wandered up to join them. "We can fit in interviews later, when there's time."

"She can interview me," Kev volunteered, stepping forward. Sabrina watched Kelly take in his 24-Hour Church of Elvis T-shirt and his Fu Manchu and suppressed a grin.

"And you are?"

"Kev Cooper, director of photography."

"The cameraman?"

"Bingo. I'm the one that makes him look good," he said, nodding toward Stef. "It's a rough job, but I'm poorly paid for it."

Stef snorted and Sabrina just kept a straight face. Kelly was looking for drama. Kev, on the other hand…Sabrina studied the glint in his eye and figured Kelly could look after herself.

"I can talk to you about the collaboration between cameraman and director. It's different on docs, you know," Kev said conversationally. "Not like regular movies, where you can rehearse and repeat a scene. Everything's spontaneous and most of it is one time only, so you've got to operate more on instinct. Now take me, I'm all about instinct."

"There you go," Stef said, "he's all yours." He picked up a light and began to walk toward the palisade, Sabrina hot on his heels.

She hustled to keep up with his careless, long-legged strides. "So you're okay about this article? If there's anything to talk about, we should do it now."

"Free press is free press." He shook his head. "You'd be a fool not to take it. With luck, my backers won't care."

"They know you've got to make a living, don't they? What, are they going to have a fit about you working on a sex documentary?"

He shrugged. "You got me. My money doesn't come from the entertainment Hollywood you hang out with." He flicked a glance at her. "It comes from grants, private donors, people who want to promote a certain view of the world. I have no idea what they're going to think about your series—or about me directing it." He set the light down next to the other equipment piled on a tarp by the wooden fence. "Anyway, it doesn't matter. I'm here and we've got a doc to film. So what are we covering?"

Sabrina dumped her satchel next to the lights. "Role-playing. Didn't you get the briefing packet?"

"Yeah, I got the briefing packet. Adults who play old-time dressup?" He gave her a pained look. "My little sister did that in third grade. What's sexy about that?"

"This is a little different."

"How?"

Her smile widened. "You'll see."

"A DRINK FOR YE, my lord?" A tavern wench greeted them with a tray of tankards. She wore a moss-green skirt and a black bodice that laced up the front with crimson cord—and stopped just underneath her breasts, which stood out round and bare.

"I'll pass, thanks."

"I think she was offering you ale, not something, um, more organic," Sabrina said as they walked away, mischief in her eyes.

"She must clean up on tips," he said, but his eyes held on Sabrina, not the tavern wench.

Sabrina wore a blue flowered sweater that reminded him of the sort Doris Day would have worn in some fifties' movie. Only Doris had never looked like this, he thought. Sabrina had troubled to fasten only three of the glass buttons, right in the center. It looked as though she'd been caught in the middle of putting it on.

Or taking it off.

Across the way in the knife thrower's booth, a woman wearing just a red satin eye mask lay spread-eagled against the target board while the knife thrower posed in a leather G-string. Stef leaned closer to Sabrina. "Let me get one thing straight here right now. No participatory segments with this one, period."

"Leather G-strings don't do it for you? I think you'd look kind of cute."

"I'm opposed to cute on basic principle, at least when it's applied to me." He rubbed the back of his neck. "So we've got a lot to cover here. How do you want to start?"

She'd begun walking off before she even answered, already caught up in the fair. "These market stalls are great. Let's see what's here before we start shooting."

Great, he supposed, was one way to describe a booth of wooden and leather medieval sex toys. He tried not to blink as a couple of customers gleefully tested out their new purchase in one corner of the shop.

And the clothing stall…all Renaissance fairs sold clothing, he figured. Just not cupless leather bras and codpieces with strategic cutouts.

In a lingerie and jewelry booth hung with velvet drapes, Sabrina held up a complicated arrangement of silver chains. "This is great," she said. "We've definitely got to get this."

He tried not to stare at her tanned belly revealed by the gap at the bottom of her sweater. "Too hard to film."

"We'll get someone to try it on, give it some contrast."

"At the risk of sounding naive, what is it?" Restless, Stef picked up a thick gold ring from a display on the counter, rolling it idly in his fingers.

"Breast jewelry." Sabrina draped it against herself.

Before he could stop it, his mind reassembled the image of her—minus the blue sweater. He remembered how soft her skin was.

"What do you think?" she asked. "We get someone to model it?"

"That would be a lovely bauble on you, milady. They're very comfortable," said the costumed clerk, sweeping her velvet cloak aside to show the intricate arrangement of gold and silver on her own—very bare—breasts, which were further enhanced by rouged nipples. "Perhaps the master will buy it for you? You can try it on for him if you like."

Sabrina locked eyes with him for a moment and a jolt ran through him. "Just looking," she told the clerk.

To keep his hands busy, Stef set the ring down and picked up another. Too big for a finger, he thought, and too heavy for an earring. Maybe it was—

"I see you've picked up one of our fine shiny pintle rings," said the clerk, materializing at his elbow. "Perhaps your lady could help you try it on."

Great, he thought. Like his imagination needed one more boost in thinking about Sabrina. He thrust the ring at the sales clerk. "Nope, I'm fine, thanks." The last thing he needed was jewelry for his cock.

Which was twitching just a bit, he realized, walking out of the stall.

"I wasn't through looking," Sabrina complained, following him. "What's the big hurry?" She took a closer look at him. "Are you blushing? Oh, my God, you are. That's priceless."

"Time to start filming," he said, checking his watch.

Sabrina just laughed. "Whatever you say." Nearby, a Lady Godiva, as naked as her reputation called for, rode a horse past the market stalls.

"Now there's a look," he said dryly.

"I think it's great. I love the fact that they get into it so much. It's more than costumes, you know. They build entire characters for these people. The whole day's scripted, if you watch."

"Like that?" He pointed to an auction block where a burly looking fellow was up for bids in a low-cut leather jerkin and pair of suede leggings split at the middle to show his hard-on. "Stud for sale?"

Sabrina shrugged. "Alternative realities," she said as a woman in a red velvet gown that laced up the front put a proprietary hand on the slave's cock.

"I guess." And Sabrina, of all people, would know. Abruptly, Stef remembered their weekends at her parents' estate—the performance artist surrounded by a firestorm of controversy for her NEA-sponsored homo-erotic art, the impassioned discussions of clothing-optional resorts and open marriage. And he remembered, oh, he remembered showing up late at a party there, hearing noises in the back and finding people running around naked. Finding her in the hot tub, with some wannabe actor's hands on her as she rose from the tub, nude. He remembered the frozen look of shock on her face just before he turned to walk away. That she could even tell him later that he was being silly, that the guy was just a jerk trying to cop a quick feel as they were all getting out of the tub, had infuriated him perhaps most of all.

He knew about her alternative realities, all right. Alternative realities of fidelity, of respect. Sabrina's idea of normal was like these people's idea of normal—tipped into another universe.

Stef took a deep breath and forced himself to release the tension in his shoulders. It was ancient history. What he had to concentrate on now was working, not the temptation in the curve of her mouth. Maybe some of his fascination for her had persisted over the years, but that was what this doc was all about—burning it out. Just as the image of her standing, naked, with some joker's hand on her breast, had scorched his hope of lasting love.

History best forgotten, he reminded himself with an impatient shake of his head. Then he offered his excuses and went to find the crew.

Setting up the lights took a little more time than he expected, mostly because Mike, the gaffer, kept getting distracted by all the bare breasts and leather harnesses. Kev just grinned and cracked his gum, watching the show as though it had been put together purely for his amusement.

"And here I always thought history was dull. I can't wait to see what our producer comes up with next."

"New York, I think, then Denmark."

Kev glanced over to where Kelly stood, talking into her handheld dictaphone as she watched Mike set lights. "If I'm going to the land of the long and the blond, maybe I should do some warmup exercises."

Stef followed his gaze. "You'll have your hands full with that one."

"Great. I'd hate to go to Copenhagen empty-handed."

"Yeah, well, get your hands on a camera first and let's take some footage."

"Whatever you say, chief."

THEY FOLLOWED THE WOMAN in red, Mary, and her new slave—in reality her longtime lover, Greg—up to the manor house. Nothing was as it seemed, Sabrina realized. Everywhere, people were playing roles and running scripts. Including the auction.

Including playing lady of the manor in an upstairs room, afterward. Tapestries adorned the walls. Candles flickered. Velvet hangings dressed the window and swooped from the canopy over the four-poster bed.

The temptation of going on camera was enough to lure the couple out of character to talk with her about bondage, role-playing and arousal.

"It's an incredible turn-on, when you know you can let go because you trust the person you're with," said Mary, lying back on the bed and sighing as Greg stroked his hands over her body. "I don't know which I like better, being the dominant or being submissive. There's something really wonderful about being tied up. I know I'm safe. I know if I say red, he'll stop everything. I'm ultimately in control, because I can say the safe word that calls it all off. But otherwise, the freedom, the exploration is amazing."

Sabrina watched Greg run the silk tassels over Mary's shoulders. "She loves the feel of the silk," he said, sliding it along her collarbone, "especially right here. I'm just sensitizing her skin a little, bringing her up." There was something so sensual about the way he touched her, Sabrina thought, something arousing about the way he knew just what she liked, the way he could speak so authoritatively about how her body worked. And he was right. Sabrina saw Mary shudder, saw her eyes go opaque with desire.

Had she ever been with a man who'd known her body like that? Sabrina wondered. Had she ever been with a man who made it his obsession to know her every sensitive spot, her every signal of desire? Then she glanced up and caught Stef staring at her, his eyes black and fathomless. Oh yes, there had been one. He'd known her inside and out, played her with a virtuoso flair until she'd been wringing wet.

"It's all about trust," agreed Greg, stripped down to his leggings. "It's about watching her body, seeing what turns her on and knowing when to stop."

Mary lay on the bed and stretched her hands toward the bedposts. At the touch of the silk ropes on her wrists, she shivered a little and stretched in arousal. "It's incredibly erotic just giving up control and worrying only about what I'm feeling," she said as her companion trailed his fingers over her nipples.

Stef watched Mike adjust the lights. It was funny, he

thought, as Kev moved in with the handheld—the couple on the bed was nearly naked and well on their way to coitus, but it was Sabrina who snared his gaze over and over. She moved back now to lean against the wall by the door, hands jammed deep in the pockets of her cargo pants, her face carved with intriguing shadows.

Not a good thing for a director, he reminded himself. He needed to focus on the subjects, not the producer. Especially not this producer, even if she had dived into the interviews as though they were the most delicious things she'd ever done, her eyes dancing.

The couple had changed places. Now Greg was tied up and Mary was crouched atop him, trailing a silk scarf over his naked body. She ran her hands down his belly, sliding them down to where his erection leaped and jerked. She ran a finger the length of it, teasing him until he groaned. Stef heard a couple of soft sighs as she slipped Greg's cock into her mouth.

Stef couldn't stop himself from looking over at Sabrina. She moistened her lips and Stef remembered how they'd tasted. How they'd felt on him. Now she stood watching the couple intently. He watched her breasts rise and fall as she took a deep breath. Raising a hand to push her hair out of her eyes, she looked at Mary's red dress where it pooled on the floor. Then she glanced up and their eyes locked.

For a long, breathless instant, the room receded. Everything else became irrelevant. Everything but Sabrina.

Then she turned and slipped out the door.

Following her was something he did without thinking. Work, he reminded himself as he stepped into the dim hallway. It was just work. But all around them, behind closed door after closed door, he could hear the sound of sex. "Where are you going?"

She stopped and turned to him, her eyes dark in flickering mock gaslight in the dimly lit hall. "I don't know. It was…I just needed a break."

"You don't like watching?"

Sabrina moved her shoulders and leaned back against the wall. "Yes. Do you?"

"There's one thing I keep finding myself watching here." Stef stepped closer. "I keep finding myself watching you." He reached out to run his fingertips down her bare shoulder.

"We're no good together, Stef." Her words were barely audible, so that he had to lean toward her to hear. The subtle scent she wore, the one that haunted his dreams, drew him nearer, and then he was too close to break away.

"I know one way we were always good," he whispered, his mouth a hairbreadth away from hers. It was a touch and not a touch, the intimacy of mingled breath, the undeniable closeness of shared heat. And it would have taken a better man than him to turn away from bridging that almost nonexistent gap.

Her flavor was hot and sweet, her mouth tempting. At first, her lips were still as though she were just absorbing the sensation, and then she began to kiss him back. He tightened at her touch, but it was the soft, involuntary sound she made that tore at his self-control. When her lips parted, he plundered, driven by the friction of tongue against tongue.

He'd never been able to entirely banish the memory

of what they'd been together. He kept expecting that the present would pale in comparison to that, but it didn't. It hadn't. The intensity that sliced through him now shocked him; the urgency catapulted him beyond anything that he'd felt before. The want, the need, the desire drummed in his veins.

He ran his hands down her flat stomach and over her hips, sliding around behind her to fit her tight against him until he could feel her breath.

Until he could feel the beat of her heart.

Behind a door someone groaned; that was followed by a woman's throaty chuckle. Down the hall, a rhythmic thud whispered of sex; a soft gasp murmured of desire. Seduction infused the air. Their straining toward each other at that moment was a reflection of the eroticism that choked the atmosphere.

Sabrina's fingers were in Stef's hair as his edged up under the thin sweater to the smooth lines of her back until she began quivering helplessly. She shivered and bit back a moan. He'd always known how to touch her— a stroke here, a brush there, a slight pressure that made her quiver.

He'd always known how to drive her crazy. A voice in her head told her it made no sense, but she couldn't seem to make it matter. It was the setting, she thought feverishly as she nipped at his lower lip, the sense that they were in a play world, that nothing that happened here could be real.

Then his hand slid further to cup her breast and she groaned. Oh, no, it wasn't play. This felt real, this heat that jolted through her. The tease of him on her tongue, the squeeze of his fingers on her nipple arrowed together to start the slow, sweet tug between her thighs. And she melted against him.

In the room behind them where Mary and Greg lay, deep throaty cries started up. The cries of sex, the exultant sound of desire made flesh. Then the shouts reached the groaning crescendo of orgasm, one before the other, before subsiding into murmurs.

Sabrina pulled away, breathing hard. "What are we doing?"

"I'd say that's self-evident," Stef replied, watching her closely.

"We've got to be out of our minds. There's a lot on the line here, too much to be messing around like this." From the room behind them came the sounds of laughter, the clicks of equipment being taken down.

"Why did you walk out here?"

"I wasn't expecting you to follow me."

"Are you sure of that?"

She stared at him, her eyes huge and questioning as the film crew stepped into the hall. "A truce is one thing, Stef. I'm not enough of a masochist to go round two with you."

Just then, Kev stepped into the hallway. "Hey, you want to come review this footage? They said if it doesn't work, they'd be happy to let us film round two."

Stef held Sabrina's gaze. "Sometimes the second time around is the best of all."

THE LATE HOUR filled Stef with exhaustion as he walked down the main staircase leading to the manor's entryway. The case of lighting equipment he carried felt like it weighed a ton. It had been a long shoot, but they'd caught some solid footage. Still, something about it felt unfinished, and his documentary habits prodded him to get more.

Below him, Sabrina reached for the doorknob, satchel over her shoulder.

"Sabrina, hold on," he called, and she turned to look at him. "I was thinking," he began and stopped, peering closely at her. "Are you okay?" She'd begun looking tired as the night had worn on. Now, though, her face was drawn and a bit pale.

"I'm fine," she replied, but she still seemed distracted. "What do you want?"

"Look, I know we've stopped shooting for the night, but I'd like to do some more. We should stay up here and catch some events tomorrow, the jousting and the human chess match. Otherwise, we're cutting ourselves short."

"We can't afford it."

"Don't need to. The owners have offered to let us stay."

Sabrina shook her head. "That's a line we don't want to cross."

"Why not? We're not filming the ranch owners, we're filming the players. Anyway, there's nothing wrong with getting close to your subjects. This isn't exactly investigative journalism. If it bothers you that much, let's get a motel."

She fiddled with the strap of her satchel. "The budget won't take it."

"Give me a break. It's twenty-five bucks a night for six people. I'll pay it out of my own pocket if you're that hard up."

"We've got enough footage, Stef. The shoot's over."

Something was up and it bothered him that he didn't know what. "With docs you never have enough footage, you should know that. Remember our discussion about you doing your job and me doing mine? Well, let me do it."

Sabrina's face set. "I said it's enough. We're not shooting tomorrow, and that's final." She looked away. "I have plans. It's a family thing."

"We'll film without you."

"Think again, Stef. It's my doc. I've got creative control."

"Then cancel your plans."

"Listen to me. We're not shooting."

"What is it? A wedding? A confirmation? What can't you get out of?"

"It's none of your business."

"None of my business? Of course not, I'm just the director…boss." He eyed her with irritation. "Why work tomorrow when you can spend the day yukking it up with whoever. The rest of us will just sit around and wait for you to get back to us."

Sabrina's voice shed icicles. "I don't owe you an explanation, Stef."

"No, but we're on a deadline here and you owe it to the project to put this ahead of some party crap."

She went white as if he'd hit her. "You have no idea what you're talking about," she said coldly, turning to open the door. "We're not shooting tomorrow. Get over it."

HE ALWAYS HAD JUMPED to the worst conclusions about her, Sabrina thought as she drove down the lit highway,

Kelly asleep in the passenger seat. She remembered that hideous day when things had fractured forever between her and Stef. He hadn't been willing to trust, hadn't been ready to understand that nothing had happened—that it was just a dip in the hot tub with friends that she'd known from elementary school, from when they'd romped on the beach in their birthday suits, practically. All except for the guest, who hadn't taken no for an answer.

Stef had been good at no for an answer. Even when his anger had evaporated, he'd been miles away from her. They were two different people, from different worlds, he'd told her. She didn't value the same things that he did. And he was doing the same thing now, she could see. He'd classed everybody at the event as "out there." He couldn't look beyond the surface and see that they were all human, that they were hairstylists and insurance agents, construction workers and computer technicians. He didn't see the role-playing as a fun part of their lives, but as what defined them.

Just as he'd always seen her environment and her friends as what defined her.

It shouldn't matter to her what he thought. So maybe for a couple of hours things had almost seemed easy between them. And the kissing…she shied away from dwelling on it. It had been a mistake. They had to find a way to work together, but that didn't mean she needed his okay for everything she did. His approval didn't matter to her, not a bit.

Besides, she had other things to think about.

8

THE NARROW OLD DINER wasn't glossy and retro like the kind you'd find in L.A. The chrome was original, though the shine had long since dulled. The red metallic vinyl seats had permanent sags from the many customers who'd plumped themselves down for eggs, bacon and coffee, staying long enough for refills. Rolando's was the kind of no-frills place that engendered loyalty, from the kind of people who came back again and again.

A waitress stopped at the table with a menu. "Coffee, hon?"

Stef nodded and watched her fill his cup. She didn't say it like she'd seen it in a movie and was trying on a role. Then again, she didn't look like she'd be taking the next day off to go to an audition. It was refreshing, he thought. Sometimes you just had to get out of L.A.

He'd woken shortly after dawn. Hit with a restlessness he couldn't name, he'd taken the top down on his Jeep and headed north along the Pacific Coast Highway. He'd cruised along the twisting road, with the sapphire-blue sea on his left and rugged bluffs on his right. Malibu had given way to Oxnard, Ventura to Santa Barbara, and still he kept going. Finally, north of Santa Maria, he'd finally stopped for gas.

Pismo Beach, the sign had read, complete with a giant concrete clam. Or oyster maybe, it was hard to be sure. At any rate, it had made him register the gnawing in his belly, so he'd tooled around until he'd stumbled on the diner.

It was Sunday, and still early enough that the place was only lightly populated. That suited him just fine. He was still disgruntled from the night before and not all that crazy about being around a crowd of people. Space and peace. It was why he'd sought the road.

That, and because he'd found himself unable to get the image of Sabrina's pale face out of his head.

"Figure out what you want?" It was the waitress.

Stef didn't bother to open the menu. "Scrambled eggs, sausage, hash browns, sourdough toast."

"Any orange juice with that?"

"Sure. You sell any newspapers around here?"

"Vending machines are just outside the door."

He fished some change out of his pocket and bought a copy of the *San Luis Obispo Sunday Tribune*. He'd driven farther than he'd realized to be out of the range of the L.A. papers.

Not far enough to get away from Sabrina, though. They'd learned years ago that they didn't fit, would never make it together. This interlude was just supposed to finish the process of clearing her out of his head once and for all. Instead, he kept coming across flashes of change in her that fascinated him. And, of course, the moments of vintage Sabrina—the mischief and fun in her eyes at the fair, the dark promise during those fevered moments in the hall.

The chalk white of her face at the end of the night.

He hadn't meant to hurt her, but to make her think. It was the way it had always been between them, no matter how she insisted she'd changed. He wanted to work and get the job done; she wanted to play. He'd been a fool to think this would be any different.

But her face haunted him.

He flipped open the paper. Out of habit, he picked out the Parade section. Though he'd probably already seen all the news weeks ago in *Daily Variety,* you never knew. Keeping up in a town built around power structures was important.

And then he saw the photo, the ripe curve of her mouth, the silky dark hair. It was longer, though, and it was a younger, much younger Sabrina who grinned up into the eyes of her father. It looked like Cannes, perhaps, or some movie premiere. The camera flashes made bright splotches of light in the background, but none of it rivaled the brightness of her smile.

The smile of perfect happiness. She'd always idolized her father. It wasn't hard to understand, Stef reflected, remembering talk of film, art and life with Michael Panotolini. The man had lived with gusto, passionate about his family and his work in roughly equal proportions. A man like Pantolini had to leave a huge vacuum behind him.

Michael Pantolini—Friends and Family Remember, read the headline. Stef froze, staring at the words, and suddenly he knew.

It hadn't been some party or premiere she'd been talking about when she'd said she couldn't shoot that day. That day, of all days.

The anniversary of her father's death.

And in an instant, Stef Costas felt like the biggest jerk in the world.

CRICKETS SANG in the late dusk. The early stars glimmered in the sky overhead, at least the few that could get past the giant pool of light that was L.A. after dark. He'd waited until then, until he thought she might be back at home. He'd come because his conscience prodded him, because his sense of justice demanded it. He'd come out of respect.

A knock at the front door brought no response. No one home, maybe…or maybe not. Brightness shone from some of the windows upstairs. And weaving through the sweet air was the slow, mournful wail of Charlie Parker. Maybe it was a neighbor or maybe not. It was worth a try, he thought. They had to get on an airplane to New York in a few days, and there was no way he'd start back into work without clearing the air between them.

Without making things right.

He headed toward the back of the house. The canal stretched out calm in the wash of moonlight. Fairy lights flickered, reflecting off of a fragmented flagstone path that traced the edge of the water. The same fairy lights traced the arches of the periodic bridges that crossed the water and connected the streets. Small night creatures aroused and chittered, and went on about their business.

A rhythmic metallic squeak punctuated the quiet setting. As Stef rounded a corner of the deck that stretched out behind the house, he saw an old-fashioned porch glider. His uncle's house had had one like that, with fat cushions and a pink-and-yellow striped canopy, the kind that swayed back and forth with just the push of a foot. And on the glider was Sabrina, alone but for a bottle of beer and the haunting strains of Parker's sax.

For a moment, he just stood and watched her. Something about the glow shot her back through the years, made her look as young as she had in the photo. But it couldn't bring back the father she mourned. It was then that Stef saw the tears on her cheeks.

"Why are you here?"

Her voice was small, rusty. She lifted the bottle and swallowed a gulp of beer.

He took a step forward, rested a hand on the railing to the steps. "I came to see how you were doing. And I came to apologize."

She was silent for a long moment.

"Look, maybe we should talk about this tomorrow. I'm going to get out of here and leave you—"

"Don't."

There was none of Sabrina's usual snap and fire in her voice, only the bit of the lost note she'd always had after waking from a nightmare. She looked at him then, her eyes watery smudges in the gloom.

He stepped up onto the deck and settled next to her.

"There's beer," she said, waving at the bottle.

He could hear the slight slur and figured that she'd probably had too much already. Maybe that was what it took, but maybe it just made things worse—dulling the good feelings with the bad. As she reached for the bottle again he stopped her, then took her hand in his instead. Her fingers were ice-cold, and he pressed them between his to warm them. She was shivering, he realized, though the evening was balmy. It wasn't physical cold. It went deeper than that.

"It must be tough."

"Always. It's…" her voice broke and she tilted her face toward the sky. "I keep…thinking that it'll get easier, you know? That as time goes by, it'll hurt less, and maybe one day this will be a time for memories and good stuff." She took an unsteady breath. "But it just never is."

Without thinking about it, Stef reached over and gathered her against him, feeling the shudder of her sobs. It always surprised him how small she was. Somehow, she had a larger-than-life quality that made him forget. Now, folding his arms around her, he felt as if he were protecting some precious gift from the outside world. He pushed back with his foot to send the glider gently rocking and made those meaningless noises that people have always made to banish the hurt and fear away.

Time slid by as he stared at the reflection of the tiny dancing lights on the water, lights that reminded him of the winking of fireflies. There was something peaceful about the scene—the arching bridges, the flagstone paths, the canoes and rowboats bobbing at the water's edge.

Sabrina stirred.

He kissed the top of her head. "I'm sorry for the things I said last night. I didn't realize what was going on."

"Why should you? Why would you?"

"I didn't mean to hurt you."

More silence. "You know the last time I talked to my father. It was about a week after you and I broke up." She sighed. "It was really ugly. I've gotten in fights before, but I've never said things specifically to hurt someone. I did that night." She was quiet for a long time, as though she couldn't stand to say the really unbearable part. "That was the last time I ever talked to him."

"But…" he stopped himself.

"But that was years before he was killed?" She gave a harsh, barking laugh. "I never meant it to be the last time. I always thought we'd make up some day. At first, I was just too mad, and after a while, it was just too easy to keep going."

"What was the fight over?"

"Me quitting film school."

It was as though she'd punched the wind out of him. She'd left, he knew, because of him. Because of their breakup.

"He'd pulled strings to get me in, made me swear I was serious. You know how much film meant to him. It was his life. When I told him I was leaving, he got so angry. It was hurt, disappointment, I know that now, but at the time…" She raised her head and stared out at the water. "At the time I couldn't see two inches past my own nose. He told me I was frivolous, useless, that I didn't take anything seriously. So I figured why not? And I spent the next three years partying. You know," she said aridly, "if you've got enough money and don't mind airplanes, you can find a party 24 hours a day." She straightened up and he let her go, all except her hand.

"When he died, it just flattened me. There was so much between us that never got fixed. And it was so bad after the funeral. They all meant well, but there were so many people around, every one of them so sympathetic it made me want to scream." Her fingers tightened on his. "As soon as I thought my mom would be okay, I got out. Drove north, up to our place in Big Sur."

He remembered it, an A-frame tucked among the redwoods and pines.

"I unplugged the phone and hid my car. I spent a week not listening to music, not saying a word to anyone, just being there in the quiet. And all I could think of was how much I'd wasted the past three years. Not just wasting the time I could have had with my dad, but wasting the time I could have spent doing what I really want to do."

"What?"

"Film. Documentaries. I came home and threw myself on Gus's mercy." She let out a long breath, no longer shuddering, just tired. "He said if I worked, he'd teach me everything there was to know about producing. That was five years ago." She closed her eyes. "You know the rest."

"No, I don't. That's all backstory, character development, motivation. The rest is what's going to happen from here on out."

She turned to look at him, her eyes shadowed. "You see why it matters, then? Why I'm serious about it? This isn't a whim, Stef. I want it more than anything. I want it to be a success. I need to prove this to myself."

"You will. You are."

"I wish…" She pushed with a foot to start the glider moving again.

"What?"

The rhythmic squeak started. "I wish he could have been proud of me."

"He is," Stef said simply, reaching over to take her hand again. "I guarantee you, he is."

9

"HERE WE ARE, a cosmopolitan, a dry martini, a Maker's Mark on the rocks, and a Guinness," said the cocktail waitress as she set the drinks down on the tiny bar table.

"Where is everyone tonight?" Sabrina asked, reaching out for her Maker's Mark.

"Oh, Delaney had a meeting and Thea's sick. I don't remember where Kelly is," Cilla said, taking a sip of her cosmopolitan.

"I think she had a premiere to cover," Trish put in.

Sabrina reached out for a cracker from the bowl of bar mix. "This might be the record for the smallest Supper Club meeting ever."

"I'm not sure we can even call it a Supper Club meeting with so few of us," Cilla agreed.

"Sure it is. It's an executive board meeting," Paige suggested. "This is where we vote ourselves raises."

"Here, here." Sabrina raised her glass to click with the others.

"Well, we might have raises to our nonexistent salaries, but how am I going to get my vicarious kicks if there's no one here to tell dating stories?" Trish grumbled, grabbing a couple of crackers from the bowl. "Delaney and Kelly always have the best ones."

"I hear someone else has stories to tell. Isn't that right, Sabrina?" Paige asked, raising an eyebrow.

Sabrina flushed and made mental plans to roast Kelly over a small fire. "Nothing much."

"Nothing like, oh, say a blast from the past?"

"Who?" Cilla asked avidly, leaning in to put her elbows on the table. She wore a white silk and lace Valentino top, with a silver globe dangling from a long black cord and jingling with internal chimes.

"Stef Costas," Sabrina muttered.

Three pairs of eyebrows shot up.

"Yes, Stef Costas," she repeated. "He's directing the documentary. He was the best person available for the job, and I went for it."

"She sounds defensive," Cilla observed.

"Bad sign," Trish agreed.

Sabrina took a long pull on her drink. "Look, it's business, okay? I tried to explain that to Kelly. There's nothing going on."

"Oh, I don't know," Paige said casually. "I hear something about a kiss that stopped traffic and a mysterious disappearance in the middle of a shoot."

"Sounds like Kelly's been talking way too much."

"No," Paige said simply. "She's worried about you and, quite frankly, so am I. Do you know what you're doing here?"

"Why does everyone keep asking me that? Do any of you? What about all the guys you date? Can you see the end of the road with all of them?"

"Well…"

"Exactly. Look, Stef was young, I was young. Things got screwed up. But we're both older now, and hopefully wiser. I don't know what that means. Maybe nothing. But he was there for me last night when I needed him. I can't hate him anymore. I don't know what I feel for him, but it isn't that."

"Oh, God," Cilla said, "she's falling for him again."

"No, I'm not," Sabrina said emphatically. "I'm going to work with him and keep my distance. I just don't want everyone to act like he's some kind of monster."

Trish nudged Paige. "She's defending him."

Paige looked at Sabrina. "Maybe," she said slowly, "he's worth defending."

"GOOD MORNING AND WELCOME aboard Flight 1584 to New York's LaGuardia Airport. Just a reminder while you're getting seated that we have a full flight today, so please be sure to place your carry-ons under the seat in front of you."

Sabrina stood in the aisle, waiting for it to clear to her row. Stef would be sitting farther back, not that she was going to look and see where. She gave herself points for having avoided him in the departure lounge. His unexpected sweetness two days earlier had comforted her, but her solitary sleep had drawn her into dreams of straining hot and wet against him and morning had found her confused and uneasy.

The unspoken agreement had been that they'd work armed and dangerous with each other. Then, the truce. And somehow, when she'd been vulnerable, the rules had changed, and she wasn't sure how to accommodate them. Somehow, even her subconscious had joined in the changing dynamic.

She shook her head as she tucked her roll-on into the overhead bin. Everyone had erotic dreams once in a while, starring the most improbable people. Just because she woke up slick and wet, with her fingertips still tingling from the feel of Stef's dream body, didn't mean anything. The fact that in the waking world she'd made a mistake and let him into her head for a moment didn't mean anything either. When she wasn't sunk in melancholy and wine, she was completely capable of controlling a conversation, and she was nothing if not good at keeping things light and superficial. It was just a day and a half in New York and then she'd be back home with some time to sort it all out.

"I swear, I don't know how you do it," Kelly said as she dropped into the seat next to Sabrina. "My blow-dryer and makeup alone fill up my carry-on. How do you squeeze everything into one bag?"

Sabrina blinked and came back to the present. "Natural beauty?" She snapped on her seat belt.

"Even you use help. Nope, I think it must be all that time you spent as a jet-setter. Or did you FedEx your luggage ahead?" Kelly asked as the plane began to roll back from the gate. "I heard that's the in thing now when money is no object."

"Money *is* an object, remember?"

"I remember, it's just not as much fun."

Sabrina rolled her eyes. "So how was your premiere?"

"Oh, fine. How was the Supper Club?" Kelly inspected her fingernails with elaborate casualness.

"Oh, we had quite a chat. They wanted to know all about Stef."

Kelly blushed. "Well, you were going to tell them sooner or later, weren't you?"

"Probably," Sabrina admitted. The airliner finished its taxi and turned into position at the end of the runway.

"What did they have to say?"

"What you'd expect. And I told them the same thing I've told you. It's history, what's going on now is business and I can handle it."

Kelly looked at her soberly. "Look, you don't have to convince me, I know you've grown up *and* you're serious about work and all that, but no one goes through what you went through and just gets past it. Don't be trying to tell yourself you can treat Stef Costas like any old guy, because if you do, you're walking around with a bull's-eye printed on your forehead."

Slowly at first and then faster, the plane began to trundle down the concrete ribbon. "Kelly, seriously, I don't think it's a problem. I've got both feet on the ground."

"It's kind of like now. You may feel like you've got both feet on the ground, but you might be starting to float a little," Kelly said as the plane lifted into the air. "Just be sure you have your seat belt fastened in case you run into any in-flight turbulence."

STEF PULLED OUT his notes on the New York shoot as the plane leveled off at a cruising altitude.

Beside him, Kev stretched and reclined his seat. "So off to New York to film a bunch of gorgeous women? I gotta say, I like Sabrina's choice of topics a whole lot more than yours, chief."

"Hey, I make docs for people who want to think with their heads instead of their—"

"I think with my head."

"Oh, is that what you're calling it now? I thought Felicia named it Oscar."

Kev raked a hand through his hair, leaving it little better than before. "Remind me never to go drinking with you again. And Felicia's history, remember?"

"So, what, you've been solo for a week now?"

Kev raised an eyebrow. "Try seven months. I know you were living in a cave while you were editing that union film, but try to keep up."

"Yeah, yeah."

"So what do you think about this whole press thing?" Kev asked. "I wouldn't think you'd want to advertise the fact that you're doing a sex documentary."

Stef shrugged. "I can't say I'm crazy about it but there's not a lot I can do."

"How about if I run interference for you?" Kev said casually.

"I don't think I need—" Stef stopped and gave Kev a narrow-eyed stare. "What are you up to?"

"Me?" Kev gave him a guileless look. "Nothing. Just trying to help, as always. Of course, if I give her a nice, in-depth interview, maybe she'll be less interested in profiling you. It'll get you off the hook."

"And give you a good reason to spend time with her."

"Hey, seven months is seven months, and she's a babe. Nothing wrong with me trying to get to know her a little better, is there?"

Stef's brows lowered. "Only the fact that she's writing a feature on this production. You screw up with her, you could screw us up."

"I'm not going to screw around with anyone." He stopped. "Well, maybe if things go well. Come on, Stef. I just want to hang out with her a little. Like now, for instance. I could spend the next five hours talking to you and watching a bad movie I've seen already." He cocked his head consideringly. "Or maybe I could persuade you to invent an urgent need to change seats with her so you can chat with our producer."

"And why would I do that?"

"Because maybe I can charm her so much she'll forget about interviewing you."

"Nice try. Next?"

"Because you really want to be up there talking with Sabrina."

Stef didn't blink. "Nice try. Next?"

"Don't think you've fooled me with that one," Kev said easily. "I see how you look at her."

"This isn't about her."

"That's right—it's about you and her."

The flight attendant passed down the aisle handing out headsets for the movie.

"Are you going to join us for the in-flight entertainment, sir?"

"Come on, you going to do it or not? I've got to make a big decision about a headset, here."

Stef eyed him. "If I do this, you'll owe me big-time."

"Yeah, right." Kev grinned. "You know what they say—the way to get what you want is by helping the person in a position to say yes get what they want."

"And I want not to be sitting next to you." Stef glanced up just in time to see Sabrina edge down the far aisle of the wide-body jet, all glossy dark hair and ripe red lips. The stewardess said something to her in passing as they edged past each other and Sabrina's laugh rang out, rich and open.

Before he knew he was going to do it, he was unbuckling his seat belt and stepping out into the aisle.

"WHAT DID YOU WANT to cover about the shoot?" Sabrina asked, reaching for her computer case. Hiding behind work seemed like the best strategy. She felt a bit as though she were exposed with no skin to protect her. He knew things about her, personal things that she'd have preferred to keep safely hidden.

And she couldn't stop thinking of the way it had felt to be gathered against him.

"We can get to that later," Stef said, laying a hand on hers to stop her. "How are you feeling?"

Heat flared up into her and she jerked her hand away. "Fine. No problem. Um, about the other night…" She hesitated. "I don't usually sit in the dark and get maudlin. You were really nice."

"Don't sound so surprised."

It almost slipped under her guard, the flash of humor that set her up for that blast of connection. If she gave in to it, who knew what would happen. Like melting ice on a river, the dislike that had helped her keep him at a distance had thinned, putting her in danger of being swept away. Talk, she thought, bring it back to an easy level.

"Well, we spent the other night yapping about me. Let's talk about you for a change. Once you get finished sullying your reputation working on a sex doc, what happens then? Do you have anything planned? You know, another significant, thought-provoking intellectual extravaganza?"

He gave her an amused stare. "I take that to mean that you're not overwhelmed by my work?"

"On the contrary, I've heard very good things about your films."

"But you've never seen one."

She rolled her eyes. "Take it personally, why don't you? Look, there are a lot of documentaries that I skip. I'm more into the light stuff. Documentary as entertainment rather than education."

"Some of us like to think they can be both."

"Sure. I'm just a bit more interested in fun than in what's good for me."

"Nice to know that some things about you haven't changed," he said, but without bite.

"Tell you what, if we get this project in on budget, I'll watch one of your docs. Maybe the next one. What's it on?"

"Greece during World War II."

She blinked and tried to muster some enthusiasm. "Oh, military stuff. Uncle Gus is into that."

He shook his head. "The underground. You hear lots about what went on in France and Denmark, and even in Germany, but you never hear what went on in Greece. My grandfather was part of it."

"He must have had some great stories."

"I never met him. He was lost during the war."

That stopped her for a moment. "What happened?"

"Nobody knows. My grandmother had gotten pregnant with my mother just about the time the Germans took over in Greece. Things got ugly pretty quick, I guess." He glanced over as the stewardesses moved up the aisle with the drinks cart. "My grandfather moved heaven and earth to get her and my uncle Stavros over to the U.S. Her family was already over here. He promised he'd follow a month or two later, but he never did."

"Did she ever hear from him?"

"A few letters for a month or two, and then nothing. By then, Greece was in such chaos that there was no way she could track him down. After the war, she waited to hear from him, but she never did."

It seemed unbearable to her. "What about the neighbors, friends, didn't they know anything?"

"All anyone knew was that he had joined the underground." Stef gave a humorless smile. "It wasn't a particularly healthy hobby."

"He was just gone?"

"People had a way of disappearing during the war. Maybe it was during some activity, or maybe the Germans found him out."

"Your grandmother must have been devastated," Sabrina murmured.

Stef nodded, his eyes sober. "I think it's always haunted her. If there's any one thing I want to do, it's to get over there and find some trace of him, some bit of information that will tell her what happened. The doc just gives me an excuse to poke around."

"And a record."

"If I find anything, it will be his memorial," he said simply.

"Have you done much groundwork?"

"I went over a year or two ago, before I started work on my last film. I've pulled permits from a distance."

"You know that Gus is Greek, don't you? He's got some cousin who's in the government. He could probably call in a favor for you."

Stef's teeth gleamed. "Why do you think I agreed to work on your project?"

"Oh." Suddenly, it all made sense.

His gaze snared hers, and suddenly her system jolted. "I don't do anything without a reason, Sabrina. Remember that."

Oh, didn't she know it. "Speaking of which, why don't you tell me what was so important that you traded places with Kelly?"

"Let's see," he said blandly as the stewardess stopped with the drinks cart. "Do you want apple juice or ginger ale?"

10

"SO WHEN WAS THE LAST TIME you came?" Annika Tudor, one of the founding partners of Candy, asked bluntly.

Sabrina blinked.

They sat in the vodka bar of the Two Sixty-Nine hotel in Manhattan. The walls curved up around them to encircle a recess in the ceiling that glowed with cobalt-blue light. Frosted glass sconces sprang up out of crumpled, honeycombed steel on the wall. The table in front of them shone clear and smooth.

Jazz played over the sound system, but the soles of their feet vibrated with the bass line of the music playing in Soma, the hotel's main bar that lay just below them. This night, Soma was the host of Candy, the monthly roving, private sex party that had become the talk of underground New York.

"I'm serious. When was the last time you came?" Annika demanded, pushing back her spill of blond hair.

"Actually, what you really should ask is when was the last time you came with someone besides yourself in the room," corrected Annika's business partner, Erin Belling.

Sabrina gave a quick shake of her head. "Wait a minute. Who's interviewing who, here?"

"You wanted to know why we started Candy," Annika said. "That's why. I mean, here we are supposedly reaping the benefits of the sexual revolution that our mothers fought for in the sixties, and it just started to seem like fewer and fewer of my girlfriends were having orgasms. Somehow, we were becoming decoupled from our sexuality."

"Uh-oh, she's going into her degree-in-human-sexuality shtick," said Erin. "The reality was that we realized that what we all wanted was a place we could be as sexy as we wanted without being judged, a place we could let loose and let go of the politics and just get…hot," she finished, trailing her fingers down the front of the leather bustier she wore. "We put the word out and set up an application to find members with the right mind-set."

"And what's that?"

"We want a club where if it feels good to you to tear your top off and dance naked, then you do it and no one cares."

"Except to egg you on," Annika added slyly.

"Any men allowed?"

"Of course. It wouldn't be nearly as much fun without them," purred Erin, staring at Mike, their young gaffer. "A guy can get in so long as he's with a member."

"And they are?"

"Women only. It sets the right tone. We figure they're probably not going to bring some guy who's uncool. We want guys who'll let loose and play, just not guys who'll go pawing members who don't want it."

"Now, members pawing guests, well, that's okay,"

Annika laughed. "Tonight's theme is Summer Strip-a-thon, though God only knows what else you'll see when we get going."

"Anni," Erin whined, "it's ten-thirty. I want to go where the good times are."

Annika rose. "We'll find you some members outside the door to interview. Come on, it's time to introduce you to Candy."

Sabrina stood and smoothed her skirt down her hips. She glanced up to see Stef watching her. Oh, that was no way to start out a night shoot, giving her looks that sent her pulse skittering. Especially a night shoot like this one.

Taking a deep breath, Sabrina gathered up her notes. Calm, she thought, professional. "Are you ready for this?" she asked Stef. In his checkerboard-patterned rayon shirt and black jeans, he looked more like a club patron than someone there to direct a film. On the other hand, she figured he'd blend in.

"Lead the way."

Kev and the rest of the crew scrambled to break down their equipment. With just a shoulder-mounted camera and minimal lights, they were ready to go.

"So when was the last time *you* had an orgasm?" Kev asked with a wink as he passed Kelly.

"Five minutes ago in the bathroom."

He did a double take. "Really?"

"I've always been coupled to my sexuality, Cooper."

"I bet," he said admiringly.

"WELCOME TO CANDY," said a blonde at the door in a shiny leopard-print bikini and gold chains, handing Sabrina a Tootsie Pop. She licked her lips and pressed a sticker on Stef's shirt that read Ask Me If I Talk Dirty. "You come and see me if you get bored, sugar," she said with a giggle.

Sabrina stepped down the short hall leading into the club and took a deep breath of pleasure as exhilaration surged through her. God, she loved a wild night out, she thought, and from the sound of it—and the looks of it— Candy redefined the word. Already, she could feel it slipping into her system—the madness, the excitement.

Music pulsed as hot spotlights shone down from above, illuminating sweaty bodies dancing in the swirl of color. The bar was a slash of blue light below, with a glowing wall of liquor behind. Whirls of neon embedded in the floor sent up halos of light.

At a glance, it looked like a typical stylish, elite Manhattan night spot.

Until you noticed that most of the women were topless. Until you saw the woman rubbing a vibrator against the mons of a dancer while a man caressed her. Until you heard the feverish auction for the guy stripping in the corner.

Oh yeah, just your typical club…with baskets of condoms scattered around like bowls of peanuts.

On a giant video screen spread across one wall, a woman leaned back and gasped as a man licked her bare breast, sliding his fingers down to the line of hair between her legs. Sprawled in chairs staring up at the film were individuals, couples and a few shifting blobs of bodies and bare skin.

She moistened her suddenly dry lips.

"Hot enough for you?" Stef murmured in Sabrina's ear. A man walking by bumped into her, sending her back against Stef, and his hands came up around her bare shoulders. "Careful, it could be dangerous in here."

Dangerous was hardly the word, Sabrina thought, struggling to get her breath. *Lethal* was more like it. Sex. It was everywhere she looked. Sex. It was part and parcel of every thought she had about Stef. Sex.

It was taking over.

Ten feet away, on a Plexiglas cube, a Candy girl and a man stood behind a dancer, slowly pulling the woman's dress up, running their hands over the exposed skin. "Candy isn't about labels and classifications," Sabrina remembered Annika saying. "Candy is just about people feeling free to do whatever turns them on for a night."

She could see how it could happen—how a person could watch for a few hours, absorb the frenzy and then find herself doing things she'd never dreamed of, stripping off her shirt and begging for a lap dance from a half-naked stranger.

Or begging for sex from the man she'd sworn she'd never want again.

"We've got our stuff back here," Stef murmured to her, pulling her over to a side wall. He leaned so close to be heard over the music that she felt the brush of his lips against her ear. A sudden shiver of arousal ran through her and she stared at him abruptly, stunned.

Stef locked eyes with her for a moment; then he blinked and shook his head. "How do you want to do this?"

Sabrina gathered her scattered wits. "Rove and get

as much as you can. Definitely get footage of the cube dancers, especially with people stripping and touching. Shoot over from that corner where you can see the film and the people in front of it. And I'd swear I just saw someone on the dance floor doing herself. Keep an eye out for that. God, we're going to get some amazing footage here, especially with all those interviews we did with people in the line."

"Got it. Mike," he barked. "Go get the rails."

"Hold on," Sabrina said, touching Mike's shoulder before turning to Stef. "What are you doing?"

"Sending him out for a dolly and a dolly track."

"No," she said, trying to ignore the woman who'd climbed on the bar to strip off her top as her audience stuffed dollar bills in her lacy bikini bottoms. "I want you to shoot it raw. I want you two feet from the woman on that bar and I want to see the sweat roll down her body."

"We're not trying to make a porn flick."

"It isn't sleazy—these are just women feeling good about themselves." The lights flashed, the music throbbed and she began to sway to the beat unconsciously. "It's okay, better than okay. We'll set the motivation with some of the stuff we got from Erin and Annika, maybe add the interview with the girl who worked for the IT company. People won't see it as sleazy, they'll see it as empowering."

"Is that how you see it?"

It wasn't a conscious decision, but instinct that had her stepping forward to meet him, nose to nose. "I see it as sexy as hell. Don't you?"

HER EYES CHALLENGED HIM, and drew him in, witchy dark and hot. All he wanted to do was obey the urge drumming through his veins, the compulsion for her that had become nearly impossible to ignore. It took all of his control, and it took time, to step back. "You want sex, we'll give you sex." Wrong answer. Like a powder flash, the image exploded in his mind—Sabrina, hot and urgent, against and wrapped around him on the Plexiglas cube.

It would have been a lot easier to concentrate on filming if Sabrina hadn't been dressed like one of the patrons in a short, short skirt and tight cropped top. She was trying to set up a rapport with her interview subjects, she insisted.

Whatever it was, it was working. He'd thought men were the ones who were supposed to be all about sex. Who knew that women were so ready to talk about it and to get out there and let loose? Sex was something that belonged between two people, he'd always thought. He still did, but there was something disturbingly arousing about the naked desire all around them, in the feverish brightness of Sabrina's eyes that told him it was getting to her, too.

They watched, they filmed and Stef thanked his lucky stars for Kev. His camera was good enough that they didn't even need the lights most of the time, making it easy to move fluidly around the room. If Sabrina wanted the sweat rolling down the breast of a dancer and onto the tongue of the man licking it, she'd have it.

And God, what he wouldn't risk to have her.

Stef stared out over the scene from the upper balcony.

The pulse of the music vibrated up through the floor and into his body; the pulse of desire pounded harder. All that she'd been to him paled in the face of who she was now. If anything, the memory of holding her in his arms on her deck had made her more real to him, had made the arousal that much stronger when it returned.

He watched her pace around the room, moving smoothly to the beat. He wondered if he'd always be able to pick her out of a crowd. He wondered at the fact that, once again, with nearly naked women all around her, she and she alone captured his attention. And he wondered, how he wondered, what it would feel like to have her clenched around him again, hot and tight and shuddering as she came.

"I'm getting some great shots," Kev said. "Mind if we stay up here for a while?"

"Sure," Stef murmured. Without making a conscious decision, he began walking down the stairs, heading toward Sabrina. In the flow of the traffic coming up the stairs, in the press of bodies, he lost sight of her.

Tension and something more primal—something like possessiveness—tightened his body. He looked toward the dance floor, where half-naked couples danced on the cubes. He looked toward the bar, where a man stripped slowly for a clutch of cheering women. And he glanced over to find Sabrina standing stock-still in the shadows under the balcony, staring across the room at the woman who sat on the table, her legs wrapped around a man who pumped his way into her, his naked buttocks gleaming.

Sabrina stood there, tense and absorbed, every fiber

of her caught up in the scene. Then, in a jolt as strong as physical contact, he felt her gaze move to him. When they walked toward each other, he registered it as surely as a touch.

He could tell himself afterward that he'd only wanted to talk with her. He could tell himself that he'd meant it to take only a minute.

But as their lips met in the deep shadows, he knew he'd be lying.

It was primal, atavistic, more animal than human. The music drummed in his head like some tribal chant. Avid and greedy, her mouth tore at his self-control. This time, finally, there was no holding back. They dove into the kiss, met and clashed, in a frenzy fueled by need too long denied. Sabrina licked at his neck and bit on his collarbone, pressing herself against him even as he filled his arms with her tight, hot curves.

On the dance floor, one of the guys stripped off his jeans with a flourish, and a woman wearing a see-through skirt over garters—and nothing else—reached out to pull down his boxers, before winding herself around him.

The image only made Stef more aware of Sabrina, of the feel of her breast in his hand, the tease of her lips.

"Haven't you ever wondered what it would be like, Stef?" she whispered feverishly, reaching down for his zipper. "Don't you wonder how it would be to watch it, to feel it, to move with it? I do," she breathed. "I do and I want you. Now."

The words snapped the final thin thread of control that held him and he backed her up to press against the wall. When her fingers pulled him out, it tore a groan from him. He kissed her lips, her eyes, then twined his fingers in her hair and pulled her head back to feast on her neck. *More,* he thought, and he slid up her short skirt to find only skin, found only her, slick and swollen and ready.

"God, Sabrina," he breathed, and it took everything he had to keep himself from letting go. Because he couldn't let go—not until his fingers were on her, not until his cock was in her, not until he felt her come.

He took the condom she handed him and slid it on. And in a push that tore a cry from him, he slid into her.

On the screen, a man sent a woman writhing with every stroke of his tongue. On the dance floor, a woman pressed a vibrator again the thinly covered nipples of another woman.

And in the corner, Sabrina braced against the wall, wrapped around Stef, impaled on his cock. The moment was beyond anything she could have imagined, the accumulated tension and arousal of years. It was an urgency that they could only have found now, when they'd come back together.

She felt the surge of him, against her and in her, his mouth on hers, his fingers, his clever fingers against her breast. He drove her, drove himself as she felt him grow thicker, harder, felt him pounding deeper into her until she was caught in the helpless chills, the glory, the blazing rush of orgasm.

THERE WAS LITTLE of the postcoital return to sanity. It wasn't enough, she thought as she felt him slide out of her. It was only a start and she wanted more.

Her feet touched the ground and she moved in for a

long, deep kiss. Let sanity wait for another time. This was a moment to savor. She sighed, leaning her chin on Stef's shoulder to stare out across the room.

Suddenly, Sabrina noticed Annika giving her the high sign, warning that either the cops or the union guys had come in. Alarm choked the glow of orgasm, leaving Sabrina shaken and focused. The four-hundred-dollar bribe she'd paid Annika hadn't been cheap, but it had been less expensive than what it would have cost to negotiate the permits and have the local unions descend on her. And if they discovered she was running a nonunion shoot, well, the price tag would rise even further.

Sabrina gave Stef a quick peck and shifted past him to hurry up the stairs, motioning Kev to cut. With this short of a shoot, and especially one inside on private property, she was willing to risk doing it bandit-style—get in and try to get out without anyone seeing, crossing her fingers that the bartenders wouldn't say anything.

Fortunately, the union man hadn't seen anything like Candy before, and it took only marginal effort—and a few Candy girls—for Annika to distract him utterly.

"Okay, get the equipment down and out of sight," Sabrina said tersely. "We're done here. Let's pack up and go."

Stef stepped in front of her. "What's the rush?"

"We have to go, Stef. *Now.*" She waited until a Candy girl had pulled the union man into a clinch and led the crew down the stairs and swiftly to the door, blowing a kiss to Annika.

Outside, it took only a minute to load the equipment into the cargo van.

"Okay," Sabrina said to Laeticia, "You get yourself

and the crew back to the hotel tonight. Make sure this stuff is crated and the alarm is on."

"I'll take my camera up to my room," Kev interrupted. "I feel better when I've got my eye on it."

"Fine," Sabrina snapped. "Then you're in charge of getting it crated and to the airport in time to ship tomorrow. Laeticia, you've got the rest of it. Low profile, everyone. You've all got your tickets for the flight home."

She listened to the doors slam and breathed a sigh of relief as the van drove off. "Now we just need to get out of here," she muttered. She glanced up to see Stef staring at her.

"What's going on, Sabrina?"

"What do you mean?"

"Where do I start? Well, hell, it's been an eventful night, but how about if we kick off with the way we just blasted out of there?"

She shrugged. "It was winding down and we've got an early flight back. Might as well head over to the hotel and relax now that all the work's done," she answered. And try to figure out just what the hell she'd thought she was doing in there.

Stef stared at her. "You didn't get a permit, did you?"

"Look, I'm really tired," she said, turning back to look for a cab.

"Answer me. If someone from the city had walked in while we were in there, you wouldn't have had a permit to show, would you?"

Sabrina let her breath out in a huff of frustration. "I already told you what it's like filming in this town, Stef. If we hadn't done it this way, we wouldn't have been able to do it at all. As it was, we had permission to be here, we ran a lean shoot and we got our footage. I don't see the problem."

"You don't see?" He whirled and walked away. "God *damn* it! You may not be running a union shoot here, but guess what? I do. You know what'll happen to my future projects if this gets out? You know how much grief Kev would have gotten, or the sound man, or the gaffer?" He broke off, stalked down the sidewalk in furious silence for a few paces and then rounded on her. "You want to take chances with your own career, go right ahead. But do not ever, *ever* do it with my crew. Understand me?"

"Fine," she bit off, flagging an empty taxi. They got in, not speaking until they reached their hotel. Not speaking even as they walked inside. Obstinate jerk, she railed to herself. He didn't understand the realities of filming and budgets and logistics. He was a classic director. All he knew was making artistic statements and leaving it to someone else to figure out how to make it work.

She slammed the key card in and out of the lock and stomped into her room, heading for the minibar. One of the small luxuries she'd allowed herself was the choice of a nice hotel in New York. With a one-night stay and a crew of six, she could afford to splurge a little.

None of those girlie drinks for her, she decided. Whiskey, straight up. She stripped off her clothes and put on a fluffy hotel robe, pacing the room, reliving the evening in her head. What she'd told Stef after the lap dance was still true—they'd always been amazing in bed. It was just outside that they ran into problems. She drank her whiskey and brooded, playing back the evening in her mind, not just the sex—she'd yet to decide whether that was cause for regret or celebration—but the discussion at the end.

And slowly, uncomfortably, she came to the inescapable conclusion that she'd been wrong. It was a valid risk—for her—but she'd had no right to put Kev and Stef and the rest of the crew in the position of taking that risk unknowingly.

It made her want to squirm. What had seemed so clear in the planning and the execution was now clearly out of line. She'd have to make a point of telling him she wouldn't do it again. That would probably pacify him. After all, what more could he expect?

She closed her eyes for a moment, then opened them and knocked back the rest of her drink. It didn't matter what he expected; it mattered what was right. It was time for a walk down the hall.

STEF STOOD AT the window, staring out into the night. He'd gotten as far as pulling off his shirt and unbuttoning his jeans before thoughts of Sabrina had him gazing at nothing. They might have ended the night shouting at each other, but it was those fevered moments inside Candy that kept playing over in his head. How could he be so furious at her and still want her so intensely?

And how, when he'd started this project to get her out of his head, had he wound up getting her so thoroughly twined into his system?

A knock echoed in the dark room, and he moved to the door.

It was Sabrina. She stood there, shoeless, in a wrinkled shirt and jeans. In the wash of light from the hallway, she looked soft, ill at ease and very, very young.

It got to him. "Hello."

She moistened her lips. "Can I talk with you for a minute?"

When he opened the door and flipped on the hall light, she stepped inside. Not far, just a step or two, to where she could lean against the wall and look at him.

She took a deep breath. "You were right about the shoot. You were right to be angry. It was a risk I was willing to take, but it was completely unfair of me to pull you and everyone else into it without letting you know. I'm sorry. It absolutely won't happen again." Her last words were rushed and she turned for the door.

"Not so fast." He put his hand on her shoulder; Sabrina froze, then turned slowly to look at him. "I came down pretty hard on you outside of the club."

"You had a right to be angry."

"It still took guts to come here and apologize," he said softly. "The Sabrina I knew before wouldn't have done it."

"The Sabrina you knew before wouldn't have done a lot of things."

"I like her better now." He slid a hand over her hair, traced his fingers under her jaw.

"This isn't smart," she warned him as he drew near.

"Was it smart in the club?" He kissed his way along her jaw, to the incredibly soft skin just below her ear.

"Things…got carried away."

"They've been carried away ever since we saw each other again," he murmured. And then he plunged them into a kiss and it didn't matter any more.

MOONLIGHT STREAMED IN the window. The occasional hiss of traffic still sounded. Sabrina stood by the bed, staring into Stef's eyes, watching him as he unbuttoned her shirt. He pushed it back off her shoulders, tossed it aside and, for a moment, just looked at her. She hadn't bothered to put on a bra just to run down the hall, and now her breasts were bare to his eyes. He reached out and pressed his fingertips to her collarbone, then traced them down, over the slight swell across the tight button of her nipple.

Sabrina shivered and reached out to touch the curves and hollows of his chest, lingering on the ridges of his corrugated belly. His breath hissed in, but still they were silent.

Slowly, he sank down to his knees in front of her. His hands, featherlight, settled on her ribs and slid down, following the line of her waist until they reached her waistband. He unfastened her jeans and slipped them off. For a moment, Sabrina wished desperately that she'd worn something more exciting than the plain white panties she'd dragged on in her room, but she hadn't thought they'd wind up making love.

Or maybe she hadn't wanted to think about it. Maybe she hadn't because she'd been afraid of what it might mean. The flash and fire of Candy was one thing; this—this silent, almost reverent lovemaking—was something altogether different.

And then Stef was pressing his face against her, kissing the flat slope of her belly and holding her for a long time. She felt the brush and warmth of his hands on her back; without thinking about it, she pressed her hands to his head. In Candy, all had been speed and intensity; now, they could savor. Time stretched out as they remained there, not thinking, just absorbing feelings that were more than sensation.

Stef shifted and his mouth was warm against the scrap of cotton Sabrina wore. Even then, it was a gently rising tide of arousal, not a storm wave, and she sighed in pleasure. Then that last garment was gone and he was pressing her back on the bed until she felt the coverlet against her shoulder blades.

When Stef joined her, he was naked and she could feel the whole length of him against her. He was beautiful, she thought in wonder, sliding her hands down his arms, over his hard-muscled buttocks, along the corded lines of his thighs. The boy he'd been had only hinted at the man, in so many ways.

Touch, taste, texture. In dreamy silence, they relearned each other. Desire quickened, but was overlain with gentleness. The quiet of the room was broken only by mouth on mouth, by the brush of hand over warm skin, by the murmurs of lovers wrapped together. And when he slid into her, it felt like coming home, as though that were the point of the journey and the tumble over the edge of orgasm irrelevant.

And then they did tumble, together, and into deep, satisfying sleep.

11

MORNING SUN SHONE DOWN through the oak and maple canopy over Central Park, dappling the paths with coin-sized spots of bright gold. Sabrina made it a game to step between the coins as she ran, the rhythmic thuds of her footfalls substituting for her fervent desire to be smacking herself upside the head.

A woman went by on Rollerblades and Sabrina stared at her enviously. If she'd been home, that would have been her, skating down the boardwalk, the sunrise on one side, the gilded waves on the other. The rush of the water and the sound of the gulls would have soothed her, the speed of her passage would have given her the illusion of escape.

Instead, she was left with just herself and the trails. Central Park was gorgeous and the pathways were beautiful, but the reality was, sooner or later, she was going to have to go back to the hotel and face Stef. Sooner or later, she was going to have to figure out just how in the hell they were supposed to go forward.

She'd been out of her mind. That was the only explanation. Some sort of a contact high at Candy, maybe. Bad enough what they'd done at the club, but compounding the error? Having a cordial relationship with him was one thing, but taking it any further was madness. Sort of like an out-of-body experience, except that her body had been involved. Very definitely and specifically involved.

She swabbed sweat off of her forehead. Maybe she should just write it off as research. She'd told herself often enough over the years that he hadn't been as good as she remembered. After all, when you had no serious basis for comparison, it was easy to put your first serious lover on a pedestal, even when it had ended badly.

And, of course, she'd wondered how it would be with him again. Any red-blooded woman would. It had been years, after all. Could he really have been as good as she remembered, and wouldn't it be worth it to find out?

Well, she'd found out, all right. She'd found out and it had been memorable. He'd polished his skills, added some control. Not that he'd ever lacked for staying power, but now he had a certain finesse, combined with some frankly fascinating new tricks. No, he hadn't been as good as he'd been in college.

He'd been much, much better.

She glanced around for cars and crossed the road to reach the sailboat pond. It would be a peaceful way to spend the day, she thought, navigating a sailboat around the water, living in a little universe she could control.

If only she didn't have to check out of the hotel to catch an early flight home.

Her mistake had been to let him sneak under her radar progressively over the past weeks. She could handle the sexy eyes and that gorgeous face, but that niceness—that fatal niceness—had been her undoing. It had been a mistake to forget their history for an instant. It was a mistake to be careless around a man like Stef.

Okay, so call it fact-finding. Call it sex in passing, nothing more. Sure, there had been something rather luscious about the feel of his arms around her as they dropped off to sleep, but there was no way she could let herself get confused. It would be positively masochistic to even think about any kind of real involvement with him. She didn't have to get flattened twice to learn that Stef Costas was bad news for the unwary. She'd learned the hard way; when it came to her emotions, he was off-limits.

Sabrina circled the sailboat pond and began heading back toward the hotel. Only women, she shook her head. Only women spent the morning after sex pondering what it all meant. Only women worried and pawed it over in their heads, trying to figure out how or if it had changed the shape of their world. Guys, they just got up, scratched their balls and headed for the bathroom.

Assuming they even got up. She guessed that Stef was probably still in bed where she'd left him when she'd sneaked out an hour before. He'd never been an early riser, even at the best of times, and he'd always slept like the dead.

She raked her hair back out of her eyes. So, fine, she'd neatly avoided facing him first thing in the morning, but she was going to have to deal with him sooner or later. Maybe she should go back, shower and go to his room—

She broke that thought off with a grimace. That was

just how she'd gotten into trouble the night before. Okay, coffee first. Once she had some caffeine in her system, she could figure something out. Neutral territory, probably, away from the hotel. They could meet at some restaurant for lunch, somewhere the rest of the crew wasn't likely to see them. The last thing she needed was to have to explain it to anyone.

Oh, who was she kidding? Kelly would figure it out with one look, if she hadn't already. Sabrina felt the tickle that told her that her eye was twitching again.

But really, though, how much harm could come of sleeping with him, so long as she put an end to it? She and Stef were both professionals. They were almost done with the project. In a few more weeks, he'd be heading off to Greece and she'd be on to other things. Really, both of them would be better off for putting this part of their past to rest. No more dreams, no more what-ifs. They'd be done with each other, really and truly.

Sure.

STEF SAT IN THE HOTEL restaurant, watching the waitress fill his mug, and shook his head at himself. Here he was, once again, sitting in a coffee shop watching a waitress pour him coffee while he thought about Sabrina. Of course, things were different than they'd been the last time he'd gone through this exercise. Back then, he'd wondered about the pull the new Sabrina had on him. Now, he'd let himself get sucked in way over his head. The hell of it was, he almost didn't mind.

"Idiot," he muttered. If it had just been the interlude at Candy, he could have chalked it up to curiosity, to pent-up desire. The fight outside the club should have reminded him of why they were bad for each other. But then she'd shown up at his door to apologize, looking so soft, chastened and pretty that he couldn't stop himself.

He couldn't chalk it up to temporary madness, because he'd had enough time to cool off. This was something that had been running through him for days, for weeks.

Maybe for years. That was what alarmed him just a bit. It was like a small temblor, that sense of something shifting just a bit under his feet, that sudden uncertainty. Alcoholics, he'd heard, could go for a dozen years without a drink, then take a sip and find themselves on a three-day bender. He knew how they felt.

Moodily, he sipped more coffee. Well, he'd wanted to get her out of his system. What did it mean that she was now on his mind more than ever? He couldn't stop wondering if things had finally changed. And he couldn't stop wanting more.

He looked up and felt something click within him. Across the room, he could see Sabrina on the other side of the glass barrier that separated the coffee bar from the main restaurant. She rubbed her temples with one hand and then glanced restlessly around. *Do it now,* he thought to himself, and waved.

She paled. He swore he saw her square her shoulders, but she got her coffee and walked through the restaurant to his table.

Working out, he figured, looking at her standing there without a speck of makeup on, her cheeks still flushed and her hair raked carelessly back from her face. The urge to tumble her back into bed took him by surprise. "Good morning."

"Good morning." She swallowed. "Having breakfast?"

"Sure. Care to join me?"

"I'm a mess. I've been running."

"I noticed when I woke up this morning," he said, his eyes on hers. "Funny, you never used to be the type to run away from things."

"I meant—"

"I know what you meant. And you know what I meant. Why don't you sit down and talk to me?"

She hesitated, then slid into the booth. "It wasn't meant to insult you. I just thought it would be easier for both of us."

"Maybe ditching a one-night stand is par for the course, but with the history we've got and our current circumstances, it doesn't make a hell of a lot of sense."

Sabrina opened her mouth to protest and then subsided, waving off the waitress with the menu. Instead, she cupped her hands around her coffee cup and stared at the rising steam as though trying to tell the future. "I was going to talk to you, just when…"

"Yes?"

"Look, what happened last night wasn't a particularly smart thing for either of us." Her voice tightened. "I mean, considering what we were filming, it's not all that surprising, but it was foolish. I think we're best off now if we just call it good."

What she was saying made sense. He should have listened to it. He wondered why he didn't. "Do you think this happened for no reason other than being at Candy?"

"No," she said slowly. "I think it's been coming on for a while. We've both been wondering what it would be like after all this time and we found out."

"And?"

"And now it's done."

Stef drummed his fingers and looked across the room, then he looked back at her. "I'll tell you what I think. I think it's very far from done. I'm not entirely sure myself what we do about it, but I can tell what I'm not going to do and that is sweep it all under the rug again."

"In case you haven't noticed, there are two of us involved here."

"Trust me, it was pretty hard not to notice that there were two people involved here last night."

A flicker of impatience showed. "Stef, last night was great, but that doesn't automatically mean we start back up again. Have a little self-control. Think how it's going to look to the crew. Besides, we have a history."

"And I think that history is precisely why we shouldn't just cut this off."

"Give me one good reason why we should keep going," she demanded.

"Because if we weren't in a public place right now, I'd have you stripped out of those running clothes so fast it'd make your head spin, and don't even pretend that you wouldn't be right there in it with me."

Her eyes darkened for an instant, then she got up from the booth. "If I were, I'd be out of my mind," she said grimly.

"Maybe…but we'd do it anyway. And we will, you know."

Sabrina pressed her hands on the table and leaned as far into his face as she could. "No, Nostradamus, we won't."

"Why?"

"Why? Because last time around, one evening in particular, you took great delight in telling me I wasn't good enough for you. And if you think that all it takes to fix that is some sympathy and a night of good sex, then you're the one who's out of his mind."

SABRINA THUMPED her makeup bag into her roll-on. Normally, travel put her in a good mood. Now, all she wanted to do was get on the plane and get home, preferably without seeing another living soul. Failing that, she'd settle for avoiding Stef. Of course, given that she and Kelly were sharing a cab to the airport with him, she'd just have to resign herself to dealing with him. It was the mature thing to do, she told herself. After all, they still had to work together. He'd realize pretty quickly that he wasn't going to get back with her and that would be that.

There was a knock. "Just a minute," Sabrina called. She opened the door to find Kelly. "Hey, come on in."

"Hi. I was packed, so I figured I'd stop by on my way down."

"Sure. I'm just about done myself."

"So how are you doing?" Kelly asked, setting her bags against the wall.

Sabrina gave her a level look. "Just for the record, 'I told you so's' are in really poor taste."

"Like I've never done something I swore I wouldn't?"

Kelly gave an abashed look. "I may give dire warnings, but I gave up 'I told you so' a long time ago." She sat down on the bed and bounced a few times. "So how was it? Did you have fun?"

Sabrina stopped and gave a rueful laugh. "You ever had fabulous sex that you knew darned good and well you shouldn't?"

"Sometimes that's the best kind of all. So what happens now?"

"Chalk it up to experience, finish the project and say night-night," Sabrina said lightly.

"I suppose if I were a good friend, I'd support you and keep my own counsel."

"Have you *ever* in your whole life kept your own counsel?"

Kelly considered. "Yeah, once. August, 1998, 2:00 p.m."

"Show me some proof and I'll believe it."

"All I've got to say is after the way he's been looking at you, don't expect him to back off without a fight."

"Everybody needs a challenge and that's mine." Sabrina zipped up her bag and grabbed her purse. "Come on, we've got to get to the airport."

Downstairs, the lobby was full of the usual midmorning chaos. Thank God for express checkout, Sabrina thought, walking past the line of people.

"So how are we getting to the airport?" Kelly asked.

"Laeticia and the rest of the crew took the van and the equipment. You, Stef and I can cab it."

They stood outside in the taxi area, waiting for a cab. "They'll be here in just two minutes," said the doorman.

"I always thought New York was crawling with cabs," Kelly said.

"It is. They're just all off crawling somewhere else."

"Speaking of crawling, where's the Greek god?"

Sabrina shrugged. "He knows when we're leaving. If he's not here, it's his problem."

"Hey, Sabrina!"

The voice came from across the drop-off area, brassy and loud. She gave a quick glance and cursed.

"What is it?" Kelly asked.

She turned in agitation. "Where's a damned cab?"

The speaker was a short, bulky man in Tommy Hilfiger, with dark cropped hair that matched his bristly five-o'clock shadow. He had the blocky-featured face of a second-rate prize fighter gone to seed, conniving and pugnacious all at once. The pitiless morning sun wasn't kind to him, she saw, bringing out a pasty complexion and puffy jowls, earned from a few too many late nights drinking, no doubt.

Wesley Franzen, ace reporter for the *Weekly News,* one of the more tawdry grocery store tabloids. The *Weekly News* specialized in dishing dirt, building stories out of innuendo, rumor and straight-out lies. She knew that for a fact—she'd been their target more than once.

"So how's your cousin these days? You still making out with him in restaurants?" Franzen asked, following them back to the taxi stand.

"Up yours, Franzen," she said over her shoulder to him.

Franzen stepped closer. "You ought to be a little nicer, Sabrina. After all, I'm the one who controls what America thinks of you."

"Civilized people don't read your tripe, Franzen."

"Are you dissing our readers, little rich girl? That's heartland America you're talking about. They're going to be very upset at you."

"Nice shirt, Franzen. It looks just like the one you threw up all over. Did you ever get the smell out of that one?"

"Bitch." His face flushed a dull red and he started after her.

"I wouldn't," said a hard voice from behind them.

Franzen blanched and Sabrina turned to see Stef standing there.

"I don't know what you're trying to do, buddy, but you'd better do it elsewhere. Now." He took a step past Sabrina as Franzen backpedaled, right into the path of an approaching cab. At the honk, Franzen tripped. He was up in a moment, dusting himself off. An ugly sneer twisted his face.

"Got a new boyfriend, Sabrina? I'm sure it'll break your cousin's heart. I'll have to keep a special eye on you now."

A cab wheeled up. "Get inside," Stef murmured to Sabrina. "I'll take care of the luggage."

Kelly and Sabrina slid into the blessed cool of the cab.

"Are you okay?" Kelly asked.

Sabrina nodded, not trusting herself to speak.

"Want to tell me what that was about?" Stef asked as he got into the cab beside her.

It still made her tremblingly angry, even though Franzen was a complete scum. She made herself take a deep breath. "Franzen hit on me at a party five or six years ago. He wouldn't take no for an answer. It got loud and it got ugly." The cab pulled out into traffic. "Later on, I came across him throwing up in a corner. Ever since, he's made it his mission to serve up sleaze stories on me whenever possible."

"I've seen you grace their cover a few times over the years," Stef said.

"He sneaked into my father's viewing and got a couple of shots of my mother. I was out with my cousin last month at a bar. Franzen got a picture of me leaning in to say something and made it look as if we were kissing. According to the story, we're having a hot and not-very-private affair. He ran it on the front cover alongside one of the pictures of my mother, saying how destroyed she was about us." Sabrina's jaw tightened. "It's one thing when he goes after me. It's another when he goes after my family."

"Take him to court," Stef said.

She snorted. "You spend a fortune, they drag your name through the muck, and if you win, there's a tiny little retraction on the last page. It's easier to ignore it." She reached out to brace herself as the cab stopped. "I was starting to think he'd given up. He hasn't done any stories for a while. Guess I disappointed him by getting off the party circuit."

"You've got better things to do," Stef said.

Sabrina looked at him with a faint smile, feeling the comforting warmth of him against her. "Yeah, I do."

12

IT MIGHT ONLY HAVE BEEN a weekday evening, but the pedestrian mall that was the Third Street Promenade was crowded with people and activity. Sabrina sat on a bench, watching a pair of street acrobats put on their show. They cartwheeled into sequences of flips, springing at the end over a low wall of cardboard boxes and rising to their feet effortlessly. Finally, one ran toward his partner and the two clasped hands just as the runner flipped up into a handstand, high above the ground on the other performer's hands.

And held it there, motionlessly, in perfect balance.

That was what she needed with Stef, Sabrina thought. Perfect balance. She needed to find some way to appreciate the kindness, work with the talent, acknowledge the past, and maintain control of the lust. Most of all, maintain control of the lust. Sleeping with him once she could chalk up to foolishness, to letting things get away from her. More than that was just walking back into involvement, and she was very afraid she was already in deeper than was smart.

Intellectually, she knew getting involved with Stef was bad news. The problem was, she'd never been one for following her head. Outside of work, her tendency was to just take the leap, to follow her whims and see what happened.

The upside-down tumbler balancing on his partner's hands wavered and drew an *ooh* from the crowd. The partner stepped a little to the left, then to the right, struggling to get under him. Sabrina felt a clutch in her stomach. See what happened? That was what happened when you went with your gut in a delicate balancing situation. One false move to upset the balance and you took a header into the bricks.

Despite his partner's best efforts, the balancing tumbler's body overtilted and he began to fall. Halfway down, though, the partner gave a swift, calculated flip of his hands and suddenly the falling tumbler pulled into a perfect tuck, spinning once, twice, and landing with grace and aplomb.

Sabrina laughed and clapped her hands as the pair took sweeping bows.

"You've got to play it for the drama," Stef said, dropping onto the bench beside her.

Though she'd been expecting him, she still jumped at the sound of his voice. "If you're a street performer, you've got to play it for the cash."

"I'll remember that. I see you've been making some notes," he said, glancing down at the clipboard on the bench beside her.

"I've pulled the permits, and arranged for the off-duty police officers and the whole nine yards. We're clear to shoot here for three hours, 8:00 to 11:00 p.m. I figure we'll catch the dinner-and-the-movie crowd, so we should have plenty of raw material."

"Any ideas about where you want to do the interviews?"

She shrugged. "Let's walk it and see."

They rose and began to amble. The Promenade was a pedestrian mall closed to automobiles, dotted with fountains and sculptures and lined with chichi restaurants and the kind of nationwide chains that styled themselves as boutiques.

"There," she pointed. "I think over by Restoration Hardware should be one of them."

"Sabrina."

She kept walking until he put a hand on her shoulder. "Stop a minute and talk to me. You've been avoiding me ever since we got back from New York."

"I've had work to do."

"We never finished talking about what happened. Or what happens now, for that matter."

"Look, you were really nice to help with Franzen and I'm sorry about the way I reacted in the restaurant. I usually have better control of my temper these days." She held his eye. "I'm not sorry for what I said, but I'm sorry for the way I said it."

"I don't care about the way you said it…" He broke off as a group of teenagers walking by jostled them. He grabbed Sabrina's hand. "We're getting out of here until we're finished talking."

At first, she only registered the feel of his skin, the contact, and all of its resonances with the other times and places he'd touched her. He steered them down a side street headed toward the bluffs overlooking the beach. Suddenly, it was a relief to get away from the mob of people, and she followed without protest. They had to get it out of the way sooner or later, she supposed. Why not now?

The setting sun hovered above the horizon. She tugged her hand from his and pulled out her dark glasses. "So talk."

"All right. You think we should end this. I think we should give it a chance."

"There is no 'it' to give a chance to, Stef. We were curious, we slept together. End of story." She rubbed her hand absently.

"No. Not end of story because I don't think either one of us is ready to just let it go."

"What, the sex or the relationship?"

"Both."

"Yeah?" She stopped by a lamppost. "Well, guess what, I am. Deal with it."

"I don't think so." He turned to face her, determination in his eyes. "The reason I don't think so is because I can feel the goose bumps," he said softly, running his fingertips up her arm. Her breath hissed in. "See, I figure if you really didn't give a damn, you wouldn't react."

She had a sudden, vivid memory of the two of them wrapped together, entirely naked and utterly abandoned. "This isn't a game, Stef," Sabrina snapped, shaking the image loose. She started walking again, toward the water and the sunset.

"If anyone's playing a game, it's you. How long are you going to go on lying to yourself?"

She rounded on him. "What makes you so sure I am? Don't come in acting like you know me better than I know myself."

"I'm not. Look, this matters," he said more moderately, "to both of us. And if we don't deal with it, we're going to walk away from this no different than we were two months ago."

"So what's the problem with that?" she challenged, crossing Ocean Boulevard to reach the railing that marked the verge of the coastal bluffs. Below, cars jockeyed for position on Pacific Coast Highway, just a stone's throw from the broad sand beach.

Stef came up to lean against the fence beside her. The sun sank toward the horizon, a golden glow of light spreading in a swath across the waves. For a long time, they were silent, watching it set. Finally, Sabrina turned to him. The ebbing light gilded her features and the offshore breeze tossed her hair. She held his gaze, eyes steady on his.

"We did this before, Stef, and it hurt like hell," she said softly. "Is it so wrong to want to avoid that?"

"No." He remembered the hurt, but he also remembered the way he'd felt that night in the New York hotel, the sense of inevitability. The sense of coming home. "But things are different now, and you know that."

"Maybe."

He blew out a breath. "Look, I'm not the same person I was back then. Yes, film is important, but it's not everything. I see that now. I can look around and want more. And you've changed, too."

He reached out and brushed gentle fingers across her cheek. She shivered. Yearning flickered in her eyes. "Don't," she whispered.

"I think about you all the time, Sabrina. I can't stop it. I can't stop wanting you. And maybe you're right, maybe it's foolish, but there's something going on here. It's not just left over from before. This is today, and it deserves a chance to stand on its own."

He leaned toward her, close enough to see the little flare of alarm in her eyes. He knew that she wanted to bolt. Instead, she stayed in place and watched him until the last minute. Then her lids fluttered shut.

The kiss was soft and light as a whisper of wind, warm against the evening air. His closed eyelids glowed red with the setting sun.

They still stood in place, Stef knew that, but it felt as though the fence had fallen away and they'd gone with it, spinning down through the air. He smelled the salt tang of the sea and felt Sabrina slide in against him.

"You can feel this coming as much as I can," he murmured.

Abruptly, Sabrina stiffened and pulled away. "But I don't want it to," she said, sudden panic in her voice. She wrapped her arms around herself, blocking him out.

The jab of hurt came as a surprise. "It's past, Sabrina. Leave it where it belongs."

She shook her head. "Easy for you to say."

"No. It's not. But I don't think we have a choice."

13

"SO THERE I WAS," Delaney said, "walking down the aisle trying to read the colors on the paint cans and— bam! This guy runs right into me."

"Literally?"

"No lie. I drop my little basket and all the paintbrushes and masking tape and knobs and dealies go flying. So I'm turning around ready to just blast him for not watching where he's going, and what do I see but this totally, absolutely, completely beautiful man looking back at me."

"Only you," said Trish, "could find a man in Home Depot."

They sat in Monsoon, among the bamboo and dangling beads, sniffing some of the best Asian food in Santa Monica.

"So what did he look like?" Sabrina asked, pulling her chopsticks out of the paper wrapper and splitting them apart.

"Redhead."

"That's unfortunate." Paige made a little moue as she adjusted the strap on her cream silk tank. "Redheads are the worst, with all that pink skin and those invisible eyelashes."

"As a redhead, I protest that remark," Trish broke in.

"Oh, you know I don't mean you, Trish," Paige said dismissively. "You're gorgeous. It's the guys. They can't use makeup and they won't use sunblock, so most of them just look parboiled."

"Not this guy," Delaney said with relish. "Dark red, more like mahogany, with these blue, blue eyes and a mouth that makes you just want to eat him up. And arms…" She sighed. "So he's falling all over himself to apologize, picking my stuff up and everything."

"Now see, how do you do that?" Trish tucked a stray lock of hair back into her clip. "If it had been me, I'd have been the one picking things up and apologizing and he'd have been gone to the next aisle."

"It's that helpless, what-would-I-know-from-running-a-marketing-department look," Cilla said dryly.

"Not at all," Thea disagreed. "I'd say it's marketing, period. She knows her clientele and she knows how to reach them."

"You're so cynical, Thea. It's not marketing, it's philosophy. Like the spiritual leader says, don't push the universe," Delaney grinned. "I just sit back and let the universe—"

"The man," Sabrina put in.

"—the man, follow his bliss. I don't force a reaction. It's amazing what happens when you let it," Delaney added as the waiter stopped at their table.

"Okay, let's see," he said, "we've got chicken satay, ahi tuna, seaweed salad and veggie gyoza." He set their appetizers on the table. "Here's a bunch of plates."

"So are you guys going out?" Kelly asked as the waiter departed.

"Let me get to the end of my story," Delaney said, picking up a skewer of satay. "So anyway, he helps me find my paint and asks me what kind of project I'm working on, and we're walking down the aisle to the end when this other guy rolls up with one of those things they carry wood on. I'm backing out of his way to let him go by when he says to the redhead, 'I got all the wood, babe. Are you ready to go?'"

A chorus of groans erupted around the table.

"You're kidding," Trish said.

Delaney shook her head ruefully. "I wish."

"They should have signs or something to warn us so we don't get our hopes up," Kelly said, picking up a gyoza with her chopsticks.

"Actually, they're a really nice couple of guys." Delaney bit into her chicken and chewed thoughtfully. "We wound up going out to lunch. They do custom furniture and they're going to help me with my refinishing project."

"I've got one that tops that," Paige announced. "I met this guy at a gallery opening last week. Jason. A little on the husky side, but good-looking. He asks me out, and he seems nice enough so I figure what the heck. We go see a flick." She took a bit of seaweed salad in her chopsticks. "Now, you know me, I like to go out afterward, talk about the movie. So we wind up at Rebecca's. The waitress comes by and he tells her he's on the Zone Diet and asks if they have any balanced meals."

"Only in body-beautiful L.A.," Sabrina said, picking up a piece of ahi with relish.

"Oh, we've still got plenty of 250-pound Bubbas sucking down pizza and beer and calling any woman who isn't anorexic fat," Delaney reminded her.

"Of course, it's just that now they're sanctimonious about it," Paige said quickly. "Jason spent the whole rest of the evening talking about how badly American people eat, and how most women don't have a clue about nutrition. He even gave me a bad time about the bread I ordered."

Trish eyed Paige's willowy figure in horror. "He can't have thought you were overweight."

"No, but he went on this rant about how women equate thin with health, and understanding metabolism—"

"And your body is a temple—" Thea added, rolling her eyes.

"—that he really, really wants to worship," Delaney finished. "That's what it was all about. He just wanted to get in your pants, so he was trying to impress you with how healthy he was."

Paige shook her head. "Up until dinner, he might have had a tiny chance of stepping foot in my house."

"But?" Sabrina prompted.

She fought a smile. "Well, as we were walking back to the car, he started talking about how tense I was, rubbing my shoulders and all. He said he knew a couple of things that might relax me, like sex, for example. That the reason eating was relaxing was because of the sensation of things touching the lips and the tongue, and that there were other ways to mimic that sensation, if I knew what he meant."

"That has to be the worst line I've ever heard," Kelly said, her expression pained. "What did you tell him?"

Paige raised an eyebrow. "I told him I was vegetarian and tried to keep meat out of my mouth."

The waiter stopped by to load more entrées on the table; for a few moments, grabbing food took precedence over conversation.

"So how's the documentary going, Sabrina?" Thea asked, passing her a bowl of chicken panang.

Sabrina scooped some of the curry onto her plate and grinned. "Great. You guys would love some of the stuff we've been filming."

"Like what?"

"People who do this whole Renaissance role-playing thing."

"I thought this was a sex documentary," Trish said.

Sabrina shrugged. "Different strokes. It was actually pretty sexy. They get out there."

"I'll say. Kev said the couple on the swing was the most out-there thing he'd ever filmed," Kelly observed, picking up some pad thai with her chopsticks.

"Is there going to be anything for the more, dare I say, pedestrian among us?" Paige asked.

"Well, we shot a segment at Candy."

A chorus of questions erupted around the table.

"How was it?"

"Did you like it?"

"Is it as wild as they say?"

Sabrina tipped her head to one side consideringly. "I don't know. Kelly, what do you think?"

"More, way more. You guys would love it. Kev said it's like a guy's wet dream of what women do when they let their hair down."

Paige studied her. "So who's this Kev?"

Kelly stirred her drink and poked at the olive with the swizzle stick. "Just the cameraman. Nobody important."

"Oh. I figured since you'd brought him up twice in two minutes that maybe he was your latest. So who *is* your Mr. Right Now?"

"Nobody."

Paige set down her chopsticks "Really? How long has it been?"

"I don't know, a couple of weeks."

Five pairs of eyes widened in shock; Sabrina just smiled. Trish spoke first. "You're kidding, right?"

"No." She took a drink of her martini.

"What, are you sick?" Cilla asked.

"No. What is with you guys? Can't I just take a break without it being a federal case?"

"Kelly's got this problem," Sabrina confided.

"And let me guess," said Thea. "This problem is named Kev."

"The guy's crazy for her, but she's playing the game."

"I'm not playing a game. I just don't want to get involved with him," Kelly set her drink down impatiently.

"Why not?" Cilla asked. "It's never stopped you before."

"He's a nice guy. I like him and I don't want to play hit-and-run."

"Just tell him you're not interested," Thea suggested.

"I've tried, trust me. He just keeps hanging around, being cute."

"It makes sense that he might not want to date anybody else while he's still hung up on you, but I'm not sure I get why that should stop you," Trish said, reaching out for her water.

"I think she's got a thing for him and doesn't want to admit it," Sabrina said calmly.

"Oh, come on," Kelly snapped, "I hardly know the guy."

"Outside of being practically inseparable from him during every shoot we've had for the last week and a half."

"So? I had to do something while you're off with Stef."

Now, five heads snapped around to stare at Sabrina.

"Well, that didn't take long, did it?" Paige observed calmly.

"'Off with Stef'?" Thea repeated. "What exactly does that mean? *Off* as in getting off?"

Sabrina huffed out an impatient breath. "I've had about all the lectures I can take on this, okay? It's not like we're back into it, hot and heavy. So we've had sex, we're talking. It's harmless," she insisted. "We finish the film and when it's done, we're done."

"Oh, yeah, there's an original one," Cilla said.

"Stop it." This time, Sabrina's temper showed. "I have to do this. You think it's just coincidence that all of my relationships have sucked since college? They've all been stand-ins for Stef. Well, maybe now I can finally break free of it."

"Hey guys," Kelly broke in, "she's right, okay?"

In the silence that followed, Sabrina shot her a grateful look.

"She knows better than us what she needs to do," Kelly went on.

"But—"

"But nothing. We've all done stuff the others haven't agreed with. Why should Sabrina be any different? It's her life. Let her live it." Kelly's voice softened. "I shouldn't have brought it up, Sabrina. I'm sorry."

Sabrina moved her shoulders. "It's all right."

"Well, it wasn't like she wouldn't have told us eventually, right?" Delaney said, adjusting the edge of her red bandeau top. "I mean, she owes us a before-and-after comparison of his performance."

Sabrina couldn't stop the smile. They went back too many years to not care what happened in each other's lives. "The earth moved. It changed my life," she said dryly.

"So, let's see, is this going to be like the end of Shrek, with the breaking of the curse?" asked Cilla.

"Yeah, but the princess turned into a full-time ogre then," Kelly pointed out.

Cilla raised an eyebrow. "Which means you might turn into a serial breakup specialist."

"Or maybe I'll just turn into someone who can have a normal, committed relationship. Look, I just need to do this. Are you guys going to stand behind me or are you going to keep giving me shit?"

There was a short silence. Thea cleared her throat. "Can't we do both?"

14

"Do I MAKE noise?" The woman gave a ripe laugh and shook her head until the beads in her braids rattled. "Kiddo, this man gets to work on me and I don't stop."

"I like it," her partner grinned, wrapping his arms around her from behind. "She starts making those little whimpering noises and I know I'm in the right place."

She gave him an affronted look. "I don't make whimpering noises."

"Uh-huh," he said into her ear. "You do like that *oh, oh* and *ooh, ooh* and *mmmm* and when you get real close, it's just a squeak."

She slapped him on the arm, blushing furiously.

"Oh, you know I be telling the truth, babe."

"Good thing you remember so well, because you're never gonna hear them again."

"Oh, I think I will," he crooned and whispered something in her ear that had her giggling. "We gotta go now, y'all," he said with a genial wave.

Sabrina looked over at Stef, who fought a grin as the couple walked out of camera range.

"That one's a keeper," he said.

She watched the quirk of humor in his beautiful

mouth and thought about the sounds that he drew out of her.

They stood on Melrose Avenue on a sweltering Saturday night. The daytime temperature had hit the triple digits, and nightfall hadn't done much to temper it. Down in Venice, it might be cool, but up in the city the heat was definitely on. Still, it made for good visuals—everything hemmed high, cut low and generally showing lots of glowing skin. The interviews would not only be fun to listen to, they'd be sexy to watch.

Still, she couldn't help staring longingly at the ice cream shop across the street. Her sleeveless linen shirt and mini did nothing to help her escape the heat. She glanced over to find Stef's eyes on her.

"Need a fan?" he offered, handing her a folded sheet of paper.

"Thanks. Next up," she called to Laeticia.

A group of middle-aged women walked up to the camera, one a zaftig blonde, one with a brunette bob and the other with a mousy brown shag.

"Okay, are you ready for some questions?"

"Ask away," said the blonde, wearing a stretchy red dress that looked surprisingly good on her. "We're all past being embarrassed."

"I'll see what I can do about that," Sabrina grinned. "So have you ever been caught in the act?"

The question provoked a chorus of laughter. The brunette found her voice first. "Oh yeah. I was about nineteen and I took my boyfriend home for Christmas, you know, meet the parents and all that. I'm sleeping in my bed and he's down on the couch. So I sneak downstairs to find him and we start making out. Well, he's got my nightshirt up around my shoulders and I kneel by the couch and start going down on him, and then I move up to kiss him. You know, following all that *Cosmo* advice."

She started to giggle and had to stop. "I guess our cat, Snowball, had jumped on the back of the couch. The way my boyfriend's cock was bobbling around when I was kissing him, Snowball thought it was a toy, so she jumped on him." The brunette stopped to get control of herself. "It didn't hurt him, but you should have heard him yell. And then when my mom came down…we broke up pretty soon after that," she added, then fell back into a fit of giggles.

"Mine is better," said the blonde. "Three words— mile high club."

"I'm almost afraid to ask," said the woman with the brown shag.

"I think we would have been okay if we hadn't hit turbulence right around the time we were both coming," the blonde said thoughtfully. "I was sitting up on the little counter with my legs wrapped around his waist, but when we bounced, I lost my grip."

"That sounds noisy."

"Oh yeah. Next thing we knew, the stewardess was tapping on the door and asking if we were all right. That wouldn't have been so bad, but then she said, 'I know there are two of you in there. I want you out of there, now. There are children on this plane.' I felt like we'd gotten caught by the teacher."

"Bet they didn't give you any peanuts during the next drinks run."

"Well, I'd already had my nuts, if you know what I mean," she said with a wink.

Sabrina paused a moment and fanned herself, then swigged from her bottle of water. Sex in an airplane lavatory. An intriguing idea. So far, she'd never been on a flight with someone she'd wanted that badly, but maybe someday. What would it be like, she wondered. Hot, hurried and desperate, probably. The very fear of discovery would make it all the more exciting. She touched her fingertips to her lips.

"Break," Stef said from behind her.

She jumped. "What?"

"We need to take a breather. It might be nighttime, but it's baking."

Sabrina checked her watch. "We need to get this footage in. The permit's only good for tonight."

"And fifteen minutes isn't going to break us. Come on."

She looked at him dubiously.

"Do I need to start a mutiny?"

"Okay, everyone, take a break." Sabrina announced and walked over to her chair. "I'll see you back here in fifteen."

"Nope." Stef took her arm before she could sit. "Come with me." He walked her over to the corner and they crossed with the light.

She matched strides with him without thinking about it. Their fingers tangled together. "Where are we going?"

"I think you could use a cooldown." He steered her to the gelato parlor and opened the door. "You've been looking over here all night, like a kid with her nose pressed up against the candy store window. I'm going to buy you a cone."

Sabrina stared at him.

"Come on," he chivied her. "You're letting out all the cold air."

She walked past him into the blessed air-conditioning. "I was debating over whether to go get the camera and get it on tape—Stef Costas taking a break from work to do something totally frivolous."

"I told you, I've changed."

The floor of the shop was a mosaic of colored tile that flowed up over the sweeping rounded counter, as though the whole thing had grown organically rather than being built. Ceramic tea sets in vermilion, cobalt, kelly green and pumpkin orange were glued to the walls. In the corner sat a giant, gaily decorated teacup, with a table sprouting in the center and a bench encircling the inside.

They got their cones—chocolate chocolate chip for Stef and raspberry sorbet for Sabrina—and walked over to sit in the teacup.

"Nice decor," Sabrina observed, taking a lick of her cone.

"Looks like they raided Disneyland."

"So the serious and brilliant Stef Costas really has learned to lighten up?"

"I told you, even I figured out that work isn't everything. It's a lot, and it's worth a lot of devotion, but there has to be something more."

"Something like fun?"

"Something like," he agreed, taking a lick of his cone.

"So it's all in the balance?" Sabrina persisted.

His black eyes were steady on hers. "Sure."

"So, in the spirit of balance and combination, I should probably get some of your chocolate ice cream to go with my sorbet. Kind of a black forest thing."

"The last person to try to steal chocolate from me was my mother," he said pleasantly. "She'll show you the scar on her hand if you ever meet her. Of course, I'm open to trades."

Sabrina licked around the bottom of her sorbet, catching the melting parts before they dripped. "Here," she held it toward him. "Have some."

"Oh no. This is chocolate ice cream with chunks of chocolate. I'm not about to trade for something as wimpy as frozen juice." He shook his head. "You've got to come up with something better."

"What did you have in mind?" Her heart began to pound just a bit harder.

"Something rich, something sweet." He nipped out a wedge of chocolate with his teeth. "Mmmm," he said, savoring it even as he watched her. "Something like this that melts in your mouth."

Mesmerized, she watched his tongue slide over the ice cream and desire swept through her. She wanted him, it was as simple as that. Maybe it wouldn't be simple later, when it was time to end it, but for now all she could think of was the way his fingers would feel against her, the brush of skin, how the sweat would taste on his neck.

Stef reached for the hand that held her cone and she caught a quick breath of surprise. Then his lips and tongue swiped over her knuckles. Sabrina's system jolted at the slick heat, her eyes wide.

"You're dripping," he said.

"GOOD EVENING TO THOSE passengers waiting in the gate area for Flight 1884 to Chicago's O'Hare Airport. Please stand by for an announcement."

Sabrina stared at her magazine. Stef was sprawled in the seat next to her, flipping through a copy of *Esquire*. She was excruciatingly aware of his presence. He reached down to tuck his magazine away in his carry-on bag and she caught a glimpse of his tanned, sinewy forearm. It sent a little flutter through her. She looked away, but not before she caught a flicker of his dark-eyed amusement.

A peal of laughter had her looking over to where Kelly sat playing cards with Kev. For someone who insisted that he wasn't her type, she seemed to be more than happy to spend time with him. Denial wasn't just a river in Egypt, Sabrina remembered Kelly's words with a smile. It seemed to be going around. Not that she was in denial about Stef, of course. She was hedonistic enough to want sex with him. It was just that her memory was strong enough to dissuade her from letting it go further.

At least she hoped so.

"Ladies and gentlemen, we've had a slight problem come up with the captain's seat in our aircraft," said the gate agent. "We've got a replacement here at the airport. We should be boarding around midnight." There was a mass groan from all of the passengers who'd begun gathering up their belongings. "Please stay in the gate area, though. If our timeline changes, we'll want to prepare for departure immediately."

"Well, hell," Kelly said feelingly, leaning back in her seat.

"No big deal." Kev glanced back down at the deck of cards he held. "We've got entertainment. Five card stud again?"

"You've cleaned me out of loose change, Cooper."

He shuffled the cards. "I take checks or credit cards."

"Not a chance."

"Euros?"

"Give it up, Kev."

He shuffled the deck elaborately with one hand, flipping segments of it around. "How about this. If you win this round, I don't bug you the whole time we're in Chicago."

"Swear?"

"Damn," he said obediently.

Kelly couldn't help smiling. "So what do you want in return?"

"If I win, you sit by me on the way."

"Look, it's a red-eye. I intend to get on that flight and go out like a light."

"Great. It'll be the first time we sleep together."

Despite herself, she laughed. "Why should I even play this hand? You've already hammered me every other time we've played."

"Because deep down inside, even though you pretend to be playing hard to get, you really like me."

"I never play hard to get, Cooper."

"I still think you like me."

"Deal," she ordered.

"LADIES AND GENTLEMEN, in just a moment we'll begin boarding our flight to Chicago. Right now, we invite anyone who needs a little extra time to board…"

Sabrina yawned and dragged a hand through her hair. She'd managed to doze off as one delay succeeded another until two hours had gone by. Now, all she wanted to do was get on the plane and fall asleep, which she figured was probably the plan of everyone in the departure lounge.

Kelly sat down beside her in Stef's empty seat. Where he'd gone, Sabrina couldn't say.

"Hey."

"Ready to go?" Sabrina asked.

Kelly looked at her, eyes bright. "Do me a favor, change seats with Kev for the flight."

"Huh?"

"Change seats. We're in the middle of a poker tournament and I'm kicking his ass for once."

"So are you guys finally getting a thing going, here?" Sabrina asked, straightening up.

"No way," Kelly said too quickly. "We're just hanging out, that's all. But you and Stef seem to be getting along okay and I figure you guys can talk about the shoot. It's not like it'll be a hardship, will it?"

Stef came up from behind them. "It will be, but I can suffer with it."

"Easy for you to say," Sabrina grumbled, giving him a look as Kelly walked off.

"They're having fun. Why not let them? Don't be afraid, I won't bite."

"Biting's not what I'm worried about."

THE FLIGHT ATTENDANTS WERE marvels of efficiency. As soon as the plane had leveled out at cruising altitude, they had, it seemed, one goal and one goal only: to dim the cabin lights as quickly as possible and put everyone to sleep. She couldn't blame them, she supposed. Sleeping passengers were happy passengers, and in the darkened cabin, most of them were well on their way.

"Well, it's the last shoot," Stef said. The reading light above drew glinting highlights from his hair, but his eyes were still shrouded in shadow and mystery.

Sabrina nodded, aware of the warmth of his leg next to hers. "Just postproduction and on to the cable network."

"And you really want to get a rough cut out in two weeks?"

"Just enough to show to the cable guys so that they can make a buy. We don't need a soundtrack and we don't need transitions." She grinned. "I think the sex will be enough to grab them."

"It always does me." He lifted up the armrests in the row and reclined his seat. "Time to get comfortable."

Sabrina followed suit, tucking her blanket around herself.

"Off to sleep?" he asked, turning out his overhead light.

"Probably not," she said. "I've been having a hard time sleeping lately. Stress, I guess."

"I know a couple of cures for that."

"I bet you do."

He reached over to punch off her light and plunge them into the dimness that shrouded the rest of the plane. "Relax. Close your eyes and I'll tell you a story," he said softly and took her hand in his.

The touch registered in her whole body. Relaxing wasn't exactly the effect. Gradually, though, the shock dissipated, replaced by a calming warmth. Bit by bit, her tension eased.

"So let's see," he began. "Once upon a time, there was this film student named Scott, who had to fill in for a sick professor."

Sabrina's eyes flew open and she stared at him.

"Eyes closed or I don't tell it."

Hesitantly, her lids fluttered closed.

"Scott was a typical graduate student, which meant he thought he knew it all. He started the lecture already planning the segments he was going to edit when class was over. It was just a bunch of freshmen, mostly bored, half-awake, looking for the easy A. He was up front, wondering why he was wasting his time, when he saw her. It was like her face was the only one he saw in the entire room. Everything else was…gone."

Sabrina lay back, eyes closed. He was just a voice and a touch in the darkness. Slowly, softly, he began stroking her hand with his finger. The touch made the hairs on the back of her neck prick up.

"It wasn't just that she was gorgeous—she was beautiful," he continued, "but there was something that brought her face alive. Life, maybe? Intelligence? Whatever it was, it totally threw him. He had to go back and review his notes before he could start again, and then she raised her hand and began to argue with him about the use of symbolism in *Citizen Kane.* And it shocked the hell out of him, but when he thought about it, she was right."

The strokes lengthened, until he was running his fingers up Sabrina's forearm with a whisper-light touch. Instead of getting used to it, she found that she felt each stroke more and more intensely. It was as though his fingertips awakened her nerve endings with every passing second, sending little chills through her body.

"Her name was…Renee, he found out later. He would have sat and listened to her just to watch her as she talked, but the things that she said, the things that she knew, blew him away."

His touch moved to her upper arm. The jolts were stronger.

"Scott had a very big problem, though, because he was her teacher, and yet every time he saw her, all he could think about was what it would be like to touch her. Fortunately, the professor came back before he lost it. That night, Scott was in his office, thinking about Renee when he heard a sound. And she was there."

Suddenly, the stroking stopped. Sabrina shivered. And then she felt his fingertips running down the sensitive triangle of skin in the open collar of her shirt. Her eyes flew open.

"So why is it we keep finding ourselves on airplanes when all I want to do is get you naked in bed and keep you there?"

She stared at him, half-mesmerized.

"Tell me we're going to do this, Sabrina," he whispered. "I've never wanted anyone as much as I want you, and maybe it's not smart and maybe we'll be sorry, but God, tell me we're going to see where this goes."

And then, hot and hard, his lips claimed hers. There was no teasing and tempting; he simply took her directly in that moment to that melting, liquefied desire. Now, she thought, and shivered under her blanket.

Oh, she wanted it. She wanted him. She could tell herself all she wanted that it wasn't smart. It didn't matter, any more than it had mattered in Candy. Right here, right now, she wanted him with the intensity of days' worth of stored desire. To be so near him, yet with no privacy, was making her crazy.

Under the blanket, his hand slipped over her thigh. Sabrina jumped. "What are you doing?" she hissed.

"Quiet, or you'll wake everyone up," he murmured, sliding his hand up farther. "We're lucky there's no one else in our row. I think we should take advantage of it."

She felt his fingers slip under the silk and lace she wore beneath her mini. The ache between her thighs intensified. The small sound of protest she made was swallowed up in the rush of white noise from the engines and the air conditioners.

"It's these skirts you keep wearing, I think. I wouldn't be nearly as tempted if you were in jeans, say, but these skirts, they just give me this irresistible urge to have my hand beneath them."

She jolted as his fingers brushed at curls of hair, then slipped in between her folds to find her slick and waiting.

He gave a soft exhalation that sounded very much like a quiet groan. "You know what it does to me to find you like that?" He dipped his fingers into her and kissed her hard.

Sabrina was drowning in the heat and the touch, amid the silent darkness of the airliner. Around them were hundreds of dozing people, blithely unaware of what was going on underneath her blanket. Stef moved his fingers up over the achingly sensitive point of her clitoris and she gulped for air, shifting against his hand. "If you keep doing that," she whispered. "I'm going to—" she broke off and gasped.

He laughed softly against her throat. "I know. I want to make you come when you can't do anything but feel it, can't do anything but take what I'm giving and go where I take you."

The words were maddening. The hot, slick stroking, that surprising, hidden flash of intimacy in the middle of the very discreet public space, had her fighting for silence. She let out a shuddering breath, her body stiffening even more as he brought her closer to the edge. Then he was plunging them into a kiss, lip and tongue, hard and deep, stroking in time with his fingers. He plunged one finger deep inside her and that was all it took to send her over, fighting to remain motionless, fighting to keep even the smallest cry of exultation within her from escaping.

Finally, she relaxed, lying limply in the seat.

He brushed his lips over hers, over her cheeks, her eyelids. Sabrina stirred and kissed her way along his cheek to his ear. "Of course, we haven't done anything about you," she murmured.

"It's different for guys, remember? We can't exactly play under the blanket."

"That wasn't what I had in mind. Three words," she said with a grin. "Mile high club."

"You remember how that story ended?"

"I think it's just a matter of avoiding the obvious pit-falls. Learn from their mistake and don't do anything that can be dislodged by turbulence." She gave him an impudent look. "Come on," she breathed into his ear. "We're three rows from the back and the flight attend-ants are hanging out in the galley up front. Everyone's asleep. As long as we're quiet…"

He reared back and stared at her, his eyes hot with excitement. "It's chancy."

"I know." She grabbed the front of his shirt and pulled him to her. "I want you inside me," she breathed and climbed over him to get into the aisle.

The half circle of rear lavatories was vacant, the lit-tle waiting area silent. During the day on a flight like this, there would always be someone everywhere, but at two o'clock in the morning, people were locked in slumber, with earplugs, sleep masks and inflatable pil-lows to make oblivion just a bit easier to find.

Stef opened the door on the central lavatory and stepped inside, turning to face the door. Sabrina gave a quick glance around and slipped in with him. When he shot the door bolt and the lights came on, the sight of the two of them together sent a frisson of excitement through her. To be in this small room, to be doing something so very pri-vate and strictly forbidden, brought on a rush of arousal.

Stef pulled her to him, and for a moment he luxuri-ated in the feel of her body against his, of having her against him, soft and yielding, and fragrant. Then the desire he'd been fixedly holding at bay twisted within him. He folded the seat cover down and sat, pushing her skirt up around her waist to catch a glimpse of the scrap of silk and lace below. Black, he saw with a swallow. The color of decadence, the color of midnight sin.

And then he pulled it aside and put his mouth on her.

Sabrina gasped as the surprising heat of his tongue bloomed through her. She hadn't thought that so soon after the last time she'd be ready, but the velvety caress had her writhing against him.

He raised his head for a moment. "No noises," he said softly. Then he bent back to his task, and she twined one hand in his hair, pressing the other against the ceiling to hold herself in place. With other men, she'd sometimes fantasized during sex to heighten her arousal. How could she ever need to fantasize now, when the very act of what they were doing was a fantasy in and of itself? When she could glance over in the mirror and see him, see herself, see them both.

Heat drove her, the slick, relentless friction of his mouth, sliding over the sensitive inner lips, dipping into her, and always, always returning to her clit. She was trembling on the edge, assaulted with chills, and still he drove her. Then she was bursting over, shuddering hard against him, against his hands on her ass. He raised his head and pulled her to him, just breathing her in for a moment.

Sabrina stirred and bent down to unzip his jeans. "Now it's your turn."

"This has all been my turn. Do you know what it does to me to make you come like that?"

"Do you know what it does to me? Shall I demonstrate?" She reached between her thighs and got her fingers slippery, then ran them up the hard length of his erection.

His breath hissed in.

"Stay quiet now," she whispered. "We don't want to get caught before you come."

Lubricated with her own wetness, her fingers slipped up and down him, over the glans, down the shaft, feeling him grow harder and harder. "Oh, I think it's time now, Stef, don't you?"

She turned around to face the door and he brought her down. The hard tip of him slid through the slippery cleft between her legs, and then she was impaled on his cock, so hard, so thick, so rough that she wanted to cry aloud. Instead, she bit her lip with desperation.

His hands on her hips, he slid her up and down until she caught the rhythm, one hand pressed against the mirror, one hand gripping the handle on the wall. It was happening again, she thought in feverish delight. The pressure, the movement, the wetness, were sending her up even as she felt him harden, heard the catch of his breath. And when she felt his orgasm burst through him, that was all it took to send her flying and shuddering and gulping for air.

And, oh, it felt so right.

"Are you okay?" Stef murmured into her ear.

"Better than okay." She wiggled a bit against him. "I'm perfect. In fact, I'd have to say this is the best flight I've ever been on."

"We try to provide only the finest service, ma'am."

Sabrina leaned back against Stef and he wrapped his arms around her. "Well, if there's anything I can do to make your flight more comfortable, just ask."

15

SABRINA PUSHED THROUGH the doors of the Chrysalis Hotel and stepped into the slate-floored lobby. On one side of the lobby, a staircase of warm wood and brushed steel curved up to the second floor. Ahead, floor-to-ceiling windows looked out onto the bluffs and the waters of Lake Michigan beyond. Sabrina turned to the front desk, toward the bearded, bespectacled man behind it. "Walt, right? I'm Sabrina Pantolini, with the documentary crew."

"Sabrina!" He stuck a hand out. "Good to finally meet you in person. So are you all set to film?"

"I don't know, are we?"

"It looks like all of the members got your letter, so no one's been surprised to hear about the filming," he said. "Everyone who's checked in so far has signed one of your releases. You folks can pretty much wander at will."

In bemusement, Sabrina listened to him outline the weekend's activities. "You'll probably want to set up for the exotic dancing contest in the lounge. That's kind of the kick-off. The action in the rooms doesn't start until then. Right now, most of them are probably still out by the pool watching the games, having cocktails." He passed her the schedule and a map of the premises.

"Co-ed naked water polo?" Stef followed her through another door and into the pool area behind the hotel.

"Hey, don't knock it until you've tried it."

The pool area was cool and secluded, protected by stands of tall shrubs backed by pines. In case that didn't dissuade unwelcome visitors, there was a discreet fence woven among the plantings. She didn't doubt that they had the occasional problem with self-appointed guests. Of course, the hotel had other kinds of protection, she reflected, remembering the security guard patrolling the parking lot.

You sort of had to, when you held a voyeurism party every month.

The broad, textured concrete apron that surrounded the pool was covered with chaise lounges, more than a few of them draped with naked sunbathers.

"Boy, I sure hope they put on sunscreen," said Kev. "Not that I'm offering to help," he added hastily when Kelly shot him a look.

The water polo game was noisy, wet and enthusiastic. It was hard to figure out who was enjoying it more, the players or the audience staring at them. This was the interplay that she wanted to get, Sabrina thought, the whole dynamic between those who liked watching and those who liked being watched. Of course, by nine or ten o'clock that night, the stakes would be raised considerably. In the meantime...

"Let's get the equipment in here and start setting up some interviews," she said briskly.

STEF HAD NEVER considered himself a jealous man, but there was something just a bit disconcerting about watching his lover interview a man whose cock was lying out there in full sight. Not that Sabrina had appeared to notice, of course, but it was hard for Stef to ignore it entirely, even if the guy was flaccid and holding hands with the woman next to him.

"So what draws you to these events, Bill?"

Bill rubbed at his blond goatee. "I like watching. I like being watched. It's a turn-on. I didn't want to come at first. I always thought it sounded hot, but actually doing it…" he shrugged. "It was Carolyn's idea to try it out."

"What do you do out in the real world?"

"I'm a business manager at an office supplies company. Carolyn, here, is an accountant."

Carolyn smiled up at the camera, her eyes hidden behind dark glasses. "It gives us a break from everyday life, you know? It's harmless. We're all here out of choice. It's not about swinging or unsafe sex. It's just a group of us that get together and do something we like."

It was funny, Stef thought. When he'd started working on the doc, he'd been convinced that most of the people they were covering were hopeless crackpots and that most of them believed in wacko alternative lifestyles that didn't make sense. Gradually, though, his thinking had changed. Again and again, they talked with people from normal, everyday life who had a different spin on things. He could see Bill playing on the local city league softball team, could imagine Carolyn driving as part of the local carpool. They weren't perverts;

they weren't underground types living on the fringes. They were the type of people you'd have for neighbors.

He signaled for Kev to do a pan of the scene. Was it that he was getting a closer look at these people or had he simply changed? He'd always considered himself a different-strokes kind of guy, but somehow the strokes didn't seem all that far out there any more.

Sabrina finished up the interviews.

"Time for a break. Take thirty, everyone," Stef said.

Sabrina touched his arm. "I'm going to go in and check some paperwork with Walt."

Stef grabbed a drink and found himself a chair at the far side of the patio, overlooking the lake. He could see why people flocked to the inn, even when it wasn't having events like this one. The view alone was worth having. He heard a noise and turned to find Kelly at his elbow.

"Mind if I sit down?" she asked.

"Go ahead."

She slipped into the chair next to him and stretched out her legs. "Hell of a view they've got here."

"I suspect it's lost on this crowd. They're too busy looking at other stuff."

"Gotta get your money's worth, I suppose," she reflected.

"Everybody's got a motivation."

Kelly turned curious eyes on him. "So what's your motivation?"

"You mean, why am I doing this doc?"

"I mean, why do you do any doc?"

Stef thought about it while he took a drink. "I guess because I like holding a lens up for people to see the world, make them look at it in a different way than they usually do."

"Like this?"

"Yeah. I think Sabrina's had the right idea all along." Now he was thinking out loud as much as anything. "Show it to people in a way that lets them see what they have in common with these people, that lets them see what the participants like and value about it. Take them on a journey. That's what docs do, you know."

"When you're watching them or making them?"

"Both, really," he said simply. "Especially when you're making them. You're not the same person at the end that you were at the beginning. You can't look at a subject this closely and come away unchanged. It's a journey of discovery."

"And what have you discovered? Apart from the fact that you and Sabrina are still compatible in bed, I mean."

He shot her a hard look. "I'm going to tell myself that one was because you care about her."

"And I'm going to keep out of it because it looks like you're there for her now. I wanted to hate you when this all started up again, you know," she said, her voice not entirely steady. "You have no idea what she went through before."

"It wasn't easy on either of us, Kelly."

"Yeah, but guess what, you're not my friend. Anyway, Sabrina's happy now, and for that I'll forgive you."

"Even though you think she's out of her mind." He said it as statement of fact.

"I think she'd be smarter if she stayed to herself, yeah."

"And is that what you do? Play it safe, stay away from anything messy?"

"We're not talking about me," she said shortly.

"Maybe we should be."

"Maybe you should stick to journeys of discovery with your documentary subjects. Tell me what you've learned from watching all of these people."

"That it's okay to risk, okay to take chances." He looked at her appraisingly. "There's a tremendous amount of trust built into a lot of these relationships, precisely because of what they're into. I've got a lot of respect for that. Risk can be a good thing, in that sense." He looked at her more closely. "What?"

Kelly shook her head. "Nothing. What else?"

"No matter where you go, there you are."

She frowned. "What?"

"Different worlds aren't so different after all. We're all much closer to one another than we think." He stirred. "Speaking of things being closer than we think, our break is over. I need to start setting up for the next shoot." They rose and turned back to the hotel. "Do you still want to do that interview at some point?"

Kelly held up her minidictaphone. "With your permission, we already have."

MUSIC PULSED THROUGH the air in the hotel's lounge, and on the catwalk of the stage, a woman wearing a red G-string flipped off her bra and threw it out into the cheering audience. She spun around the brass pole, then licked her finger and trailed it up her body, over her breast to the nipple. Heaven only knew who she was in real life, Stef reflected, scouting the room for a new camera angle before indicating a spot to Kev and Mike. That, he guessed, was part of the pleasure.

The stripping contest was down to the final few contestants. When the last round was over and the awards were given, that was when things were supposed to really heat up. Already, audience members were quietly slipping out the door.

Kev nudged Stef. "So you're down to your last chance. You can still sign up to compete. Let your johnson get a little fresh air."

"Why not you?"

"Naw." He settled his eye against the viewfinder of the camera. "I keep mine for private showings only. It's kind of shy. Not like this crowd."

No, shy would never be used to describe them. It was an odd mix, though, Stef noticed. Most of the audience had at least some clothing on, though many of the women wore outfits that would be considered indecent elsewhere. It was almost as though they understood that a pretense at clothing and modesty was more erotic than out-and-out nudity. Even the woman on stage had kept her G-string on until the very end of her dance.

He felt a touch on his shoulder and Sabrina was behind him. "Are you just about done here?" she said into his ear, taking the opportunity to give him a surreptitious kiss. "Kelly says they're already starting up in the rooms."

Kev turned to give Kelly a speculative look. "You been doing some recon?"

"Just wandering around," she said blandly.

"How about if Sabrina and I go do some recon," Stef suggested, ready to have her to himself for a while.

"Sure thing, chief," Kev said and he just kept filming.

KELLY BARELY NOTICED them leave as she stared at a couple in the back row making out with abandon. The woman had her hand in the guy's pants and was obviously handling him. "Looks like some people aren't waiting for the rooms."

"I guess they don't appreciate patience and finesse the way some of us do," Kev said, panning the camera to catch another woman on the catwalk, this time in a leopard-skin bikini and gold body paint.

"You, finesse?"

"I'm all about finesse, not to mention discretion. This filming naked women thing really isn't my bag." A corner of his mouth twitched.

"And here I figured you'd be thinking you'd died and gone to heaven—all this skin, all this sex."

The contestant on stage finished to a round of applause. Kev lowered the camera and looked at Kelly. For once, the dancing light of humor was gone from his eyes. "Random sex and random skin gets old, just like anything else. I'd rather find something real, with someone who thought I was worth breaking the rules for."

Kelly blinked and moistened her lips. "You know we can't get involved. I'm a journalist. You're one of my subjects."

"Rules, again?"

"They're generally there for a reason."

"Sometimes. And sometimes they're just bullshit to

hide behind. You going to go on hiding, Kelly, or are you ready to take a risk?"

Tell me what you've learned, she heard herself asking Stef.

That it's okay to risk, to take chances.

She swallowed hard and watched the MC put a ribbon around the neck of the winner. "I'm ready for this documentary to be over."

SABRINA AND STEF walked around the luminescent blue of the pool and toward the rooms that opened onto the patio. Each room ended in a wall of glass fitted with a slider, affording the occupants an unimpeded view of the pool area and the lake beyond. Now, however, the direction was reversed. The draperies that usually provided privacy had been drawn and the glow of lamps brought the focus inside.

The idea was not for those inside to see out, but for those outside to see in.

A knot of people had gathered around one of the rooms, standing inside the open sliding glass door or peering in from the outside. Dressed in royal blue, the bed was lit like a stage set. The scent of incense drifted out into the night air. And on the bed, Sabrina could see the gleam of naked bodies entwined.

It took her by surprise, the impact of the image. She had, on one or two memorable occasions, seen an adult film. It hadn't seemed sexy; instead, it appeared somehow vaguely foolish. The fake moans and groans, the slapping together of body parts in improbable positions—it had all just seemed silly.

What was in front of her, though, did not. These two people were obviously into what they were doing and, more obviously, they were into being watched while they were doing it.

Someone, she saw, had set up a video camera in the room so that the couple could see themselves on the television even as they were the center of attention. A little thrill of excitement shot through her. She turned to Stef—

And found him watching her. For an instant, the intensity in his gaze robbed her of words. Desire. It was in the taut, stripped-down lines of his face, in the tension coiled in his body. It vibrated through the air between them.

On the bed, the woman moaned as her partner used his hands and mouth to coax her toward orgasm. Her hips rose, her fingers clutched at his shoulders.

Sabrina swallowed. "We should set up a shot to get the bed and the television screen. It's really hot."

Stef swept her in close to him. "You're hot," he murmured.

The cries behind them rose. "We can't do this now," Sabrina said desperately. "I want you, but…"

He gave a growl of frustration and pulled her in for a deep, hard kiss. "I know. I'll wait," he said, releasing her. "Okay, how do you want to set it up? Are you sure you can get away with showing this?"

She moistened her lips. "Sure, as long as we don't show actual penetration. I don't want it to focus on the bed action, though. I want the people watching, and I want the video display."

"The video display?"

"Look at the couple on the bed. They're watching themselves making love while other people are watching them."

His hands were back on her, a warm temptation. "And you like that, don't you?"

"Yes, I do," Sabrina managed. She leaned back and gave him a long look. "I like it a lot."

Stef let out an unsteady breath. "Okay, let's get this damned thing filmed so we can get out of here."

THE DOOR OPENED and Sabrina and Stef half fell into their room, clutching and clawing at one another. It had seemed endless, but their work was done, their night just beginning. Sabrina threw down the things she carried; she thought Stef might have tossed his camera on the bed. It didn't matter. Nothing mattered except that they were free to touch, free to feel, free of worrying about anything except the madly spinning whirl of desire that had swept them up.

"If you'd gotten us rooms at the Chrysalis instead of here, I could have had you naked and coming by this time." Stef tugged her stretchy T-shirt off over her head and fastened his mouth back on hers. The tension and arousal of the past hours, tension they'd done their best to put aside, drummed insistently for release.

"Too much money," Sabrina panted, unzipping his pants. "Besides, I figured we'd need a break from the constant sex."

"Don't think you're getting one anytime soon," he growled, unclasping her bra and pulling it off of her shoulders.

Sabrina gasped at the feel of his tongue, the scrape of his teeth against her nipples. "That's all right. It'll help us get in touch with our subjects."

"I'll settle for getting in touch with you," he murmured, steering her back to the bed and laying her against it to strip off her thong. He nibbled at her knee and began to kiss his way up her thigh.

Sabrina reached out to grab a handful of the coverlet and hit the video camera instead. "Stef," she managed.

"Mmmm."

She felt the vibration of the sound against her skin and fought not to moan.

"Did you bring the video camera for what I think you did?"

"An experiment in getting closer to our subjects," he murmured. Then he went to work with his tongue and her hips rocked.

"Getting closer how?" she gasped.

"Don't interrupt me. I'm busy," he said, and then she didn't have the presence of mind to interrupt him because the stroke of his tongue and the heat of his hands on her breasts bounded her world, binding her in tension and pressure and heat, compressing her down into a single spot until all the tension burst outward, shooting through her entire body until all she could do was gasp and shudder.

Stef kissed his way up her torso until he lay alongside her. "You seemed fascinated by the video setup at the Chrysalis. I was wondering just how fascinated."

"Very." Sabrina nipped at his lips and then leaned in for a long, mindless kiss. It was a chance to explore, a chance to be safe, a chance to go with him to the edge.

Stef rolled her over onto her back. "Fascinated by the idea of watching us make love? We can do it, you know. We can do it right now."

HE'D GUESSED RIGHT, Stef realized, watching her eyes darken.

"Yes," she whispered. "Only I don't want to stop."

"It'll only take a minute, I promise."

He rose from the bed and picked up the camera and walked over to the lowboy dresser that held the television. He plugged the cable into the back, then picked up the video camera and squinted at it.

"You're so sexy when you get all techie," Sabrina murmured, coming over to kneel in front of him. She reached out to wrap her fingers around his cock. "I don't want you to lose interest while you're doing it, though," she whispered, and slid him into her mouth.

Heat, softness, slick friction. A measured caress that had him sucking in a breath. For a moment, he didn't want to focus, didn't want to concentrate on anything but the sweet, hot stroke that was slowly driving him mad. She gave a chuckle deep in her throat and the vibration of it threatened to send him over.

He'd watched the people in the rooms that night. He'd stared at the avid eyes of the voyeurs, poised on the edge of coming just from watching. He'd seen the sex-blurred eyes of the exhibitionists, closer to orgasm because they knew others could see what they were doing. Through it all, he'd thought only of Sabrina, wanted only her. Seeing all the naked limbs and smelling the rising scent of sex had only made him want her wrapped around him, somewhere quiet and private, just the two of them. Somewhere they could take one another to places they'd never been.

At the instant before the point of inevitability, he put a hand on her head to stop her. "Go over onto the bed," he said, his voice strained. He turned the camera on, aimed it across the room and then turned on the television. The image of the bathroom door popped up on the screen.

Sabrina stood up and kissed him.

"Are you sure you want to do this?" he asked. "There's no tape in it—it's just displaying the scene on the monitor."

"I want to watch us," she said, her eyes bright. She reached out and shifted the camera on the bureau, aiming it toward the bed, then she stepped in for a long, hot kiss, twining her tongue around his. "And I want you, on the bed, on your back."

"Yes, ma'am."

He lay down across it and she crossed the mattress on her knees, unable to resist bending over to taste him one more time, glancing up to see their images on the screen. It was a private voyeurism, a way to watch and be watched that included only the two of them. Her arousal pitched higher.

Stef made a sound of frustration. "Why don't you come over here so I can reach you?"

"I've got a better idea." She straddled him and slid herself back and forth on the hard length of his cock a few times, until she could feel the flush of arousal coming on, until she could see his jaw clench. She leaned in for a kiss, then she rose just a bit so he could reach himself. She could feel the tip of him rub against her and she gave a little moan. Then he pumped his hips up. The sensation of his erection driving into her, deep and hard, tore loose a cry she didn't know she was capable of.

And from somewhere, the madness came, the pent-up desire from all they'd watched. His hands were on her breasts, her hips, driving her motion. Then he flipped her over so that she was on her back and he was on top of her. Suddenly, the monitor was forgotten, and all she could see was the tight purity of his face as his pleasure gathered and he surged over the edge, dragging her with him.

16

"I DON'T KNOW WHY you didn't hire caterers, Cilla," Kelly grumbled, fishing sticks of chicken satay out of the broiler and setting them on a serving dish.

Cilla threaded chunks of meat and bell peppers onto a skewer. "I figured having an honest-to-God barbecue would give the guys something to do. Keep 'em out of our hair while we gossip."

"I thought we wanted them in our hair," said Delaney. "Wasn't that the whole point?"

"We're appealing to their caveman instincts—meat, fire, women." Cilla set the finished skewers on a platter and started up another.

"My mother always said that the way to a man's heart was through his head and his cock," Delaney said, adjusting the neckline of her little flowered sundress.

"Wow, she really said that?" Sabrina looked interested.

"Well, technically, no. She said the way to a man's heart is through satisfying his appetites. I just extrapolated."

"Hell, the way to *my* heart is through food and sex," Kelly muttered, picking up the satay platter and heading out the door with it.

"She forgot the sauce." Sabrina picked up a dish

of peanut dip and bowl of tortilla chips and went after her.

Outside, the night was balmy and clear, with a light breeze to tease the flames of the tiki torches flickering around the backyard. The blue glow from the pool lit up the dozen or two guests milling around. The task had been for each Supper Club member to invite one female friend and one male friend, with the request that each of them do the same, and so on. Given how early it was, it looked like they were on target for a good crowd.

Sabrina caught up with Kelly at the food table. "Hey, you forgot the sauce."

"I knew there was something I was missing." Kelly bent over to get a beer, her stretchy black-and-white op-art skirt riding up dangerously in the back.

"Careful there," Sabrina said, standing behind her. "I think I just saw your tonsils."

"Sorry, Mom. Does that mean you don't want one of these?"

"Not at all." Sabrina grabbed the bottle opener from the table and cracked open their bottles. "May the road always rise to meet you." She clinked her bottle against Kelly's.

"So how's postproduction going?"

"Not bad," she said bemusedly. "It's funny. I was so prepared for it to be a battle, but somehow we both have the same vision for what the end product should be, and Stef's got much better instincts for getting there."

"That's encouraging. Maybe he learned a thing or two during the filming."

"Maybe we both did."

Kelly drank and stared across the pool meditatively. "I miss being on the shoots, you know? It was exciting. I can see why you like it. I'm going to have to propose more on-site features."

"Don't expect them all to be like *True Sex*."

Kelly laughed. "Trust me, darlin', short of a porn movie, I don't think any of them could be quite like *True Sex*." She quieted for a moment. "It was just fun hanging around with you guys all those days. I miss the crew," she said wistfully, and hesitated. "I miss Kev."

"I wondered."

"More fool me. I figured I'd get him out of my system pretty quick after things were over with. I even went looking for a guy to have a fling with, but I just couldn't get into it."

"Why not try a fling with Kev?"

Kelly sighed. "I don't think it would be that easy. You can't have a fling with someone when you know them well enough to care about what happens."

"Some people would say that's the only time you should have one," Sabrina said dryly.

"Maybe." Kelly took a meditative drink of her beer. "Maybe."

"GET A LOAD of this street," Kev said, as he drove his mint-green Corvair through the Brentwood neighborhood. On both sides of the street, manicured lawns ran up to an eclectic collection of polished houses. The boulevards were broad, that itself an extravagance in an area with some of the highest property values in L.A. Turn-of-the-century oaks and eucalyptus nodded over the houses. Discreet signs warned of high-tech security systems. Beverly Hills might have been showy, the Westwood Corridor might have been chichi, but in Brentwood, money was discreet.

"By the way, thanks for the invitation," Kev said, drumming his fingers on the steering wheel.

Stef watched the house numbers. "I figured I'd better get you out before that sad-sack look on your face became permanent. The way you're moping around all the time, *I'm* starting to get depressed."

"I never mope. I'm just being…thoughtful."

"Is that what you call it? No wonder I don't pay you to think."

They drove past a house clotted with cars. "That it?"

"Yeah. Park anywhere would be my guess. So don't you have another one of those panty hose commercials to shoot?"

"Yeah, so?" Kev drove to an open stretch of curb.

"Well, that should cheer you up. The last time you did one, all you could do was gush about the talent they've got modeling the goods. If you're going to get thoughtful, I'd figure that would be the one to get thoughtful about."

"Nah." Kev dismissed it. "Not my type." He looked over his shoulder and backed the car snugly into place.

"Since when are beautiful redheads not your type?" Stef stared at him and then opened his door. "Or are you more into blondes these days?"

Kev scrubbed a hand through his hair, leaving it more spiky and disordered looking than ever. "It doesn't matter. Let's go meet some new women. Whose party is this, anyway?"

"One of Sabrina's friends. I'm supposed to meet up with her here and catch a ride home."

Kev looked around as they walked up to the front of the extravagant thirties-style bungalow. "Nice digs."

"I'm sure she'll be happy to hear that you approve," Stef said dryly. He knocked on the door and waited, but no one answered. "The address is right," he muttered.

"Oh, just open the damned door. There are too many cars here for it not to be the party." Kev reached past him and turned the knob just as the door opened up to reveal Kelly.

"Hi, Kelly. Good to see…" Stef's voice trailed off when neither she nor Kev moved. It was interesting, he thought looking from one to the other. He'd never quite seen so well-matched a set of poleaxed expressions.

"What are—"

"It's good—"

They both stopped and just stared at one another. Stef eased past them to get through the door. "Well, I can see you guys have things to talk about. I think I'll just go find Sabrina."

And if they needed any more of a nudge than that, he thought, they were beyond his ability to help.

Stef walked from one room to the next, searching for Sabrina. Only a handful of people were around, none whom he recognized. It was later than he'd thought, it seemed, judging by the ravaged table of food in the dining room.

The house was one of the type once common in L.A.—hardwood floors, coved stucco ceilings, clever niches and cutouts between rooms. He crossed under the archway that divided the dining area from the kitchen. The glow of lights and sound of voices outside caught his attention. Through the kitchen window, he could see the pool area, complete with patio, landscaping and colored spotlights.

And a steaming hot tub.

His jaw tightened and he consciously released it as he searched out the slider that would let him out onto the patio. He just needed to find Sabrina and everything would be fine. A glance around the handful of people in the backyard didn't reveal her. He started for the hot tub. Steam rose from it, twining around the heads and shoulders of the people inside. He saw what he thought could be the back of Sabrina's head, but couldn't discern details.

Then she turned around.

"Stef!" She rose and he stopped in his tracks. It was a trick of the light, he told himself. It was a trick of the light, because there was no way she'd be in that tub nude with all of those people, not after all they'd been through.

He hesitated. He thought he saw some expression flit across her face, something like hurt, then she was climbing out of the tub, tugging at the sides of her bikini bottom. Because she was wearing a suit, he saw, it was just a peachy tan that, in the lights, had blended with her skin tones.

"Gee, Stef, you look surprised. What, you thought I'd be tubbing alfresco?" There was a little wounded note in her voice that grabbed his gut and made him ashamed of himself.

Sabrina picked up a towel from a pile on the patio table and wrapped it around herself. "You're late."

"I got held up trying to get some paperwork finished that they need in Athens tomorrow." He stepped in to kiss her. "I brought Kev. I thought it might cheer him up."

"You know Kelly's here."

"I figured."

She raised an eyebrow. "That should be interesting."

"My thoughts exactly."

"You always play matchmaker?" she asked.

"Never. Hell, I can't even figure out my own love life most of the time. The last thing I want to do is try to mess around with anyone else's."

She gave him an indecipherable look. "Well, maybe we should get you a drink and you can drown your sorrows."

"I didn't mean—"

"Later, Stef," she said sharply. "This is a conversation we don't need to have right now. Why don't you come on over and say hi to the rest of the gang?"

THE HEADLIGHTS of Sabrina's car strobed across the front of Stef's house as she pulled to a stop in the driveway. "Well, here you are, home safe and sound," she said brightly.

"I think we can count on that." Stef paused expectantly. "Aren't you going to turn off the engine?"

Sabrina reached out to adjust the air-conditioning vent. "I thought I'd go home for tonight."

"Don't," he said softly. "Come in and talk with me."

"We've been talking all the way here."

"Sure, about the new Gehry retrospective, and how tacky you think the new Jaguar looks, and how much you like Paige's new boyfriend. Pretty much about everything except what's really bothering you."

"There's not a whole lot to say, Stef. I saw the look on your face tonight. I know what you were expecting, which was a little hard to choke down. I guess I hoped that by now you'd trust that I'm not the same person I was back then. It shouldn't have been a surprise."

"It wasn't. The whole scene just took me back, that's all."

"To that night in college? Forget it, Stef. *I* have."

"You haven't forgotten it any more than I have. We're both carrying it around or we'd be in the house instead of sitting in this driveway."

Sabrina was silent for a moment, then reached out and turned off the ignition. "Fine. Let's go inside and talk."

She'd never been in his house before. Perhaps because his offices were close to Venice, they'd always wound up at her place. Now, she looked around at the clean industrial styling, at skylights, hardwood floors, dramatic modern art on the white walls. It looked more like an art gallery than a home.

"The deck on top has a view of the Pacific, if you want to go up there," Stef said diffidently from the kitchen.

"This is fine," she said and crossed to the sofa. The curved triangular top of the blond wood coffee table before her held a bowl of colored glass spheres. "You've got a nice place here. I didn't realize documentaries paid so well." She sat down and ran her hand along the satiny wood.

"It's a matter of making the right choices." He walked up the stairs and handed her a glass of wine.

"Making choices. You always were good at that. Like when we broke up. I never quite knew what happened. One minute, things were fine, and the next, we were over. Poof. No explanation, no dialogue. Just a decree."

"I couldn't figure out how to explain it all then. I didn't think you'd understand." He stayed on his feet, moving restlessly, around the room. "I've only started to understand it myself."

"So try me now."

Stef stopped and turned toward her. "I guess I owe you that." He looked down into his glass. "I suppose it starts with my grandmother. She raised me, mostly. I mean, my parents were around, but they worked a lot. So she took care of me."

"What did they do? You would never talk to me about any of it." Her glass of wine sat untouched.

"I was still really angry at them then. Business development, management. They're both fast-trackers, quintessential yuppies. Good enough people, I guess, they just should never have had kids. I see that now that I'm grown and they're more friends than parents." He wandered over to the freestanding marble-faced fireplace that separated the living room from the dining room. "I mean, it's not that they didn't love me, but I think my mom decided to get pregnant mostly because she read all the 'have it all' books. She got married, got her MBA, and a baby was just part of it.

"And then, suddenly, she had this squalling little creature who wanted her attention when she needed to work overtime to finish a business plan and get that promotion. So she managed me like she would any other project—she delegated. I reported to my grand-mother—work, achieve and stay out of the way."

Children learned what they lived, Sabrina thought. When goals were all you heard about, they became all that mattered. "How did your parents react when you told them you wanted to go to film school?"

"About the way you'd expect," he said dryly. "It was a foolish idea, I'd never make a living, I was chasing pipe dreams. At first, they refused to pay for it. They finally agreed to cover it if I double-majored in business, but only if I made dean's list throughout."

"I remember you working like a dog. Doesn't sound like much fun."

"It wasn't. Then you came along." He looked at her then and crossed to the couch to sit beside her. "You were such an enigma to me when we first met. You were the exact opposite of what I'd always been—doing everything on impulse, always chasing after fun. And yet you were smart, you were talented. I'd watch you and I couldn't understand it. My MO was set a goal, make a plan and follow it."

"I remember." Though she'd never understood it, until now.

"It drove me crazy, the way you just nonchalanted your way through life, and yet I kind of envied you. You had this gift for letting go effortlessly, for not worrying about the consequences, and somehow everything always seemed to fall into place for you. Me, all I ever did was think about consequences and what happened next. And your family…"

"Ah yes, my family."

"They made me miss mine," he said simply, picking up one of the glass spheres.

She frowned. "They don't seem very much like the picture you paint of your parents."

"Not my parents. My other family. My mother's obsession was blending in, getting ahead, making money. She, my dad, both worked so hard to escape the ethnic neighborhood, to hide the fact that they were children of immigrants." He rolled the glass sphere around in his hands. "But my uncle Stavros was just the opposite. For him, it's always been all about family. I used to go visit for a week or two every summer and it was something else. Big, noisy, chaotic…they had six kids, not counting all of the second cousins and great-aunts in the area who'd come over on the weekends. Never a quiet moment. Everybody had an opinion and they weren't shy about letting you know it. And God forbid if a kid was disrespectful. But any little thing one of us kids did— hitting a baseball, carving a stick—you'd have thought we hung the moon. And laugh? God, they laughed. Your family reminded me so much of them."

"My mother asked about you at first, after." Sabrina hesitated. "It was hard."

"I've missed her, too."

She leveled a look at him. "But you knew I wasn't stepping out on you with that idiot in the tub."

"I'm not sure what I knew back then," he said frankly, "except it ripped me open to see a man with his hands on you. And it didn't seem to bother you at all."

"Because it didn't mean anything."

"To you, maybe. But it did to me, and the more I thought about it, the more it meant. Everything was just so easy for you, everything was about having fun."

"Stef, that's what you do at nineteen."

"That's what you did—but I couldn't." His expression tightened. "Not with my parents threatening to pull the plug at the slightest whiff of failure. Even my grandmother was always on me about getting a real job and getting married and having a mess of kids like my uncle. 'Why don't you find a nice Greek girl? Why don't you get out of that place and come back to a decent city?'"

He leaned forward, resting his arms on his knees. "When I saw you getting out of that hot tub that night, it shocked me. Maybe it shouldn't have, but it did. And yeah, it pissed me off that you were naked with someone you hardly knew, that what we were together didn't mean more than that to you. God, Sabrina, we'd been talking about moving in together."

She remembered the look of disgust on his face as she'd risen from the tub, and she remembered going after him, just a towel wrapped around her. "I was with people I'd known since kindergarten," she said, hating herself for sounding defensive. "Everybody but that one guy, and he was Rob's roommate. I felt safe. I didn't realize I'd get left alone with him, or that he'd paw me. And I didn't realize how you'd take it."

"That was it—you didn't know. Maybe looking back it's easy to see why that was. But the whole incident made me see how different we were. I mean, here I'm working my ass off trying to stay in school while my grandmother, the only person who really showed any interest in me growing up, is telling me to settle down with a nice Greek girl, and you're hot-tubbing naked because it's no big thing where you come from—which suddenly looked like some other galaxy. And I couldn't see how who you were and where you came from could ever fit with who I was and what I wanted.

"And it hurt like hell. So I had to make it stop."

The remembered hurt of their breakup shivered through her. She stared at him as he sat in silence. "You were pretty harsh about it."

"How do you speak when you're convinced you don't know the language? Or when you're not sure the other person even cares?"

"Of course I cared. How could you not think I wouldn't after all the time we spent together?"

"Because you were the girl in the hot tub—and I was the guy who did nothing but work. And that seemed to sum it up right there."

If they were talking about a past that was dead and gone, how was it that she was fighting back tears? "So that's how you think of me—some spoiled, rich, party girl?" She stared at the ceiling until she was sure she could talk. "That's not what I was then, but afterward? After you left, I made a career out of it." She remembered it all—the endless flights; bouncing around from resort to resort; the nameless, faceless, gutless people she spent years of her life hanging out with. "The thing is, everything becomes boring if you do it long enough. Somewhere along the line, you find yourself just going through the motions." She shook her head. "That's what

I realized after my father died. We've talked about this already. I thought you understood."

"I do," he murmured.

"So, then what were you thinking tonight at the party?"

Stef looked down at their intertwined fingers. "I guess I just had a flashback. I know you've changed, Sabrina. I can see it. You don't have to feel like you've got to prove it, least of all to me. It's just…you've had five years to watch this happen. I've only had a month, plus what I read in the newspapers. It takes some getting used to."

"You followed me in the newspapers?"

He scrubbed his hair out of his face. "Pathetic, isn't it? Every time I opened a magazine or looked at an entertainment section, you were there—off in that galaxy of yours. And I'd see your face and tell myself I was just going to page by, that we were done and over and it didn't mean anything. But I'd always find myself turning back to read it. And it used to make me so damned mad to see you trivializing yourself, because I knew you were capable of so much more. And it used to make me crazy that no matter what I did, I couldn't get you out of my head."

"Well, nothing I tried worked with you, either." Her voice was wry.

"You couldn't have seen me in the paper."

She flicked a glance up at the ceiling. "That didn't help. I didn't want to think of you. I told myself you were just some jerk of a film student. I told myself you didn't matter."

"And what do you think now?"

She leaned over and pressed her lips to his.

"That's not an answer."

"I'm not sure I have one," she said slowly. "This feels good and it feels right. I think that has to be enough for the time being."

17

"Uncle Gus?"

"Well, here's a surprise!" Gus Stirling rose and walked across his office to envelop Sabrina in a bear hug. "Are you sick of running your own show? Want to come back to work for me?"

She grinned. "Nope, we're in the middle of postproduction. I've got plenty to keep me busy. But, Gus, look." She handed him a videotape with a hand that hardly shook. "It's the rough cut for the pilot."

His eyes widened. "Congratulations! This calls for a celebration. I think all I have is some Junior Mints. The doctor told me to stay off alcohol and caffeine."

"That sounds like a misery."

"Not necessarily. I think I'm happier now that I can sleep through half of the boring meetings I get stuck in." His teeth gleamed in a smile. "So, what do you say? Can we watch the tape?"

"I was hoping you would. This is your copy. I'm taking the other one over to the Home Cinema studios right now." She watched him turn on the television that sat in a corner of his office and stick the tape into the VCR. "I figure I'll give Royce Schuyler a peek, see if we can't close on some business on the basis of this one."

She sat next to him, her palms damp, as the opening animation sequence flashed on the screen. Somehow, she was more nervous in front of Gus than she would be in front of a stranger. Gus would be a good test of whether the doc worked or not. She'd get an honest opinion and, she prayed, a positive one. She so wanted him to be proud of her.

The tape was still raw, with no links between segments and much of it missing a sound track. Still, Gus watched it intently. When he laughed at the right spots and whistled at others, she began fractionally to relax. The final segment ended in an abrupt cut.

"We'll have closing credits here. We're going to link the segments with street interviews and short animation bits." She cleared her throat. "What do you think?"

He picked up the remote, shut the VCR off and then straightened up and looked at her. "I think you've got yourself a hit."

"You really like it?" she asked anxiously. "You're not just saying that?"

"I really liked it. I think it has just the right tone— fun, funny, insightful. It's more than just sex. You and your crew have put together quite a package."

"Oh, Gus!" She rose to wrap her arms around him.

Gus beamed at her. "That's my girl. I knew you could pull it off."

"On time and on budget," she said proudly.

"I expected nothing less. How did the filming go, by

the way?" His voice took on an innocent tone as he set the tape to rewind. "Your crew work out okay?"

Sabrina eyed him narrowly. "Work out in what context?"

"I know you had reservations about Costas. I was just curious about how it went."

"Well, everything wound up being fine. You were right, of course—he was perfect for the doc. It'll be hard to find a follow-up act for him, but the pilot establishes the style of camerawork and the framework for the production.

"You can't get him to stay on?"

He had no idea how difficult a question he was asking. "He's got the Greek shoot to do, remember?"

"No way you can postpone your series?"

Sabrina snorted. "Not if I'm lucky. We'll see what Schuyler has to say, but I'm hoping they'll come in with a buy on the basis of the pilot. It's going to be a hustle as it is to get enough segments together for the spring season. I couldn't possibly wait for him. As it is, I may need to set up two separate film crews to get it all done."

"Well, if you'd wanted something easy, you'd have stayed working for other people."

She raised her eyebrows. "Is that a polite way of saying I'm a masochist?"

"No," he said, "it just means you don't shrink from a challenge. You're your father's daughter, all right."

"Am I, Gus?"

"He'd have been proud of you, that's for sure." Gus crossed to her and rested his hands on her shoulders, smiling. He kissed her on the top of the head. "Now, go sell that pilot to Royce Shuyler."

STEF SLOUCHED in the chair in front of the editing machine, running through the footage Sabrina had chosen from the street interviews. It was his job to winnow the segments down further, choosing the montages that would best bridge the gaps between segments. When the office intercom beeped, he picked up the phone without looking. "Yeah?"

"Gus Stirling is out here to see you."

Stef blinked and stopped the editing machine. Funding sources always took priority, especially when they were friends. He stepped outside of the darkened editing room, squinting at the light. "Hey, Gus, good to see you." They shook hands, Stef marveling as always at the strength of the older man's grip. "Still keeping up with your tennis, I see."

"Wouldn't miss it."

"Come on in," Stef said, waving him into his office. "Have a seat. So what can I do for you?"

"Oh, I was in the neighborhood and figured I'd stop by."

Gus never just "stopped by." Stef looked at him warily. "Did you get the budget sheets from Mitch?"

Gus sank down in the visitor's chair. "A few days ago."

"A few days ago?" Stef frowned. "We've had them finalized for a couple of weeks."

"I got to be quite good friends with his secretary before I managed to get him on the phone directly."

Stef made a note to himself on the pad that sat by his telephone. "If you have problems getting things from him in the future, just let me know. I'll take care of you. The question is, do the numbers work for you?"

"Well, you know my philosophy as an investor," Gus said comfortably. "You find a worthy project and then you trust the team to do their job. If you feel like you've got to monitor them every step of the way, then you've probably picked the wrong team." Gus gave him an affable smile. "Judging by the numbers, it looks like you folks have got everything in hand. When do you head to Greece?"

Stef checked the calendar on the wall. "In just over two weeks. We'll take a week to prep once we get there and start shooting right after."

"Good. I saw the rough cut of Sabrina's documentary, by the way."

Here it was, Stef thought, the real reason for the old fox's visit. "What did you think?"

"Well, it needs finishing, obviously, but it's a good piece. I really think they're going to go for it."

"Do you think it'll win an audience?"

"Hard for it not to, don't you think? There's always a fascination about sex—what people do, what they don't do. People can't resist finding out what their neighbors are up to. Oh, I think it'll gain a following, all right."

"Good," Stef said in satisfaction.

"You came through on our bargain. I owe you one."

"You don't owe me a thing, Gus. You pulled me out of a hole by coming through with the financing. It was my pleasure." It was more than a pleasure; it had changed his life. If it hadn't been for Gus and his ideas, Sabrina would have remained a taunting memory, instead of becoming something more.

Whatever that was.

"What did you think of my goddaughter?" Gus asked, as though he'd been reading Stef's mind. "As a producer, I mean."

Stef leaned back in his chair. "I thought she was good. Seriously good."

Gus nodded. "I told you. She's been working hard for a lot of years to get to this point. She's pretty well held every job in the line. It's hard to argue with that kind of experience. She's not just a pretty face, although she certainly is pretty. Mind you, I'm biased." He paused.

Stef fought a smile. He'd never been pumped in quite so discreet a fashion. "You'll get no arguments from me." And precious few details, also. He doubted that Gus would be thrilled to hear about his goddaughter joining the mile high club, for example. Still, he'd throw him a bone to make him happy. "If I thought that Sabrina would be satisfied working on my kind of doc, I'd try to get her on my team. As you're aware, my producer has his moments."

"Have you talked with her about it?"

"They're really not her kind of thing, Gus. Besides, if this *True Sex* series takes off, she'll have her hands full with that."

Gus steepled his fingers together against his chin. "I've always been a believer that you should never rule anything out without exploring it."

Oh, he'd be quite happy exploring Sabrina, Stef thought. "Maybe sometime in the future."

"You never know, maybe in the future she'll have partnered with another director and you'll have lost your window."

In a different way, that was exactly what was concerning him. Not that he'd have lost his window to work with her, but that he'd lose his opportunity to be with her, period.

Gus checked his watch and rose. "At any rate, I've got a lunch appointment to get to, so I'll let you get back to the editing. You've done some good work for my goddaughter," he said as they shook hands. "And you may not call it a favor but I do, and I won't forget it."

Stef showed the older man to the door and walked thoughtfully back into his office. What Gus had said was inescapable—the window was closing on his time with Sabrina.

The question was, what happened now? According to the schedules, he'd spend another two weeks working postproduction and then leave for Greece. The filming there was currently scheduled to last four to six months, by the time he finished with all of the sites and the interviews. He sighed. The problem was, it was the worst possible time to leave. Nothing had been settled between them. Sure, they'd established that they had feelings for one another, but that was about it. Sabrina was still skittish and he wasn't entirely clear himself on how they would make things work, only that he was pretty sure he wanted to.

Canceling the Greek shoot wasn't an option. The window there was also limited, and too much time and money were already involved. So he basically had three options. He could go off to Greece leaving things as they were and hope to pick it up when he returned, assuming she hadn't gotten involved with someone else. Or they could have a serious talk before he left and try to keep things going via phone and e-mail.

Or he could ask her to come with him. Things were on hiatus with her project until she got a firm deal with the cable network and the money came through. She could come to Greece and stay, even for a couple of weeks, for as long as her schedule was clear. If he posed it to her as a collaboration, it wouldn't come off as if he were expecting her to chase him around the globe or as if he didn't respect her career. He'd be asking her to come along because he valued the skills she'd bring to the project. Maybe he'd even offer her one of his percentage points.

No, it wouldn't be Mykonos and all the glamour she was used to, but that wasn't what she was about anymore. She'd told him that she'd given up party time and he believed her.

He rose to return to the editing room and sighed again. He could splice film to make a story turn out any way he wanted. Why couldn't he do the same thing in real life?

HIS SHOULDERS AND NECK were tight from the hours of hunching over the editing machine, but Stef had most of the street interview segments cleaned up. It was a good day's work, he thought, rubbing his trapezius muscles. Maybe someday he'd get that computer editing system and give up his trusted methods.

There was a brisk rap on the door and Sabrina burst in, grinning madly. She wore a dress of some silvery fabric that laced up the sides and flapped around her upper thighs in a fringe.

"They *loved* it!" she burst out as he rose from his chair. "I showed Schuyler the rough cut and he liked it so much he dragged a couple of the other programming guys in to watch!" She threw her arms around him and gave him a great smacking kiss, then danced him in a circle.

"That's great!" Stef squeezed her and then whirled her around for the sheer joy of it.

"Oh, it's the best! You can't imagine." She bounced on her toes. "They want to buy the pilot on the basis of the rough cut. He said they're going to meet on the series, but he expects them to make an official buy as early as next week. Oh, Stef, there's no way it would have been this good if it hadn't been for you and your crew."

"Hey, you were the one with the idea. We just executed it."

"And that's the part that counts," she reminded him. "You've put so much of yourself into this. I don't know how to thank you."

"Remember, there's a long way to go from a rough cut to a finished product," he warned. "I'm not going to finish the postproduction before I leave here. You've got a lot more work to do."

"I know, I know, I know, but the important thing is that they liked it so far." The delight on her face was infectious.

"Well, you look like you're dressed to celebrate. Where do you want to go?"

She stopped, then visibly gathered her wits. "Well, actually, I can't, at least not tonight," she said rapidly. "Remember? I'm going to that premiere with Matt."

"Matt?"

"My cousin? Remember, his new shoot-'em-up is coming out?"

The disappointment was thick and baffling. "Oh, right."

"I shouldn't cancel. I haven't seen him in ages and he's promised to introduce me to a couple of people who might be interested in getting in on the financing of the series. I need to schmooze. Besides," she twirled around, "I'm in the mood to celebrate. You can meet us at the party if you want."

Something twisted in him. "I doubt I'm on the guest list," he said quietly.

"That doesn't matter. Matt's got an open pass everywhere in this town."

"I should probably stay here and finish cutting the street interviews," he said. "We can go someplace tomorrow."

A trace of concern crossed her face and then it brightened. "Of course, anywhere you want." She crossed over to hug him tightly. "I've got to go. Thank you, Stef, really." He felt her body mold to his briefly, then she drew away. "I'll call you tomorrow," she said over her shoulder as she left, trailing stardust.

It didn't matter, he told himself, refusing to let the doubts surface. It didn't change anything.

He wanted so much to believe he was right.

18

"TELL ME AGAIN what I'm doing in Vegas when I really just want to be at home rolling around in bed with you?" Stef asked, standing at the closet door of the hotel room. He looked back to where Sabrina stood by the bed in garters and a demibra, rolling a stocking up her leg. God, it was maddening to know they'd have to spend the night in public. He wanted to ask her the question that was burning him up, he wanted to strip her back down to nakedness and make love, just as they'd finished doing a half hour before. Instead, he was watching her dress. "Why are we doing this?"

She fastened the front garter. "Because the National Cable Show is going on and Home Cinema is having their reception. They want to court the local cable providers and that means trotting out programming execs and stars to make them feel important. We're part of the team now, so we give them what they want."

"And we count as stars?"

"You're always a star to me, darlin'." She looked down, focusing on fastening the back garter.

He walked over and pressed a kiss to the nape of her neck, making her jump, and then captured her mouth with his for a moment when she looked up in surprise. "And can I tell you that it's only because I'm enthralled with you that I'm doing this?"

"Thank you for your sacrifice." She rolled the other stocking up her leg.

"I don't suppose I could talk you into just staying here? I'm sure we can find a way to keep ourselves entertained." He reached around and filled his hands with her breasts.

She softened against him for a moment, turning back to kiss him. "I'd like nothing better."

"Room service, champagne, take that hot tub for a test run…" And they could talk about the future. Even if it was only for a short time before her project got rolling, he wanted her to come to Greece with him. He was impatient to make the step, to invite her into his life.

"Mmmm, sounds wonderful." She turned back to finish her garters. "Tomorrow. Tonight, we work."

She slipped out of his arms and strode over to the closet.

Stef stifled his impatience. She was wary, he knew it. And he knew his younger self was to blame. Now that it was so apparent that they were right for each other, it was hard for him to wait for her to see it, too. Seven years before, he'd complained that she was too frivolous. How was it that now he was frustrated that she was putting work ahead of play? He didn't need to set the scene, what he was going to ask was going to be simple enough. He should just do it.

He walked restlessly over to the wall of windows overlooking the grounds. "You know they have a pool here with a wave machine? In the middle of a desert?"

"Have pity on the Philistines, Stef," she said dryly. "Just think, this time next month you'll be in Greece, without over-the-top kitsch or a schmooze fest in sight." Sabrina lifted a deep copper silk dress over her head and shrugged her shoulders so that it slipped down around her body to brush at her thighs.

"No little black dress."

"Copper is the new black, or so Cilla says." Sabrina slipped on a pair of strappy copper sandals and glanced at herself in the full-length mirror on the closet door.

"So what's the plan? Do they have a program or screenings or what?"

"Or what, mostly. The execs have been in meetings all day. Now, they want to party. There'll probably be some sort of entertainment and clips of shows, but mostly it's a giant love fest," she said with a light laugh, coming over to peck Stef lightly on the lips before turning into the bathroom area.

"What about your doc, are you on the schedule?"

Sabrina searched in her makeup bag for an eye pencil. "Just a teaser, but every little bit helps."

"You're good with the details like that." She heard the clink of his belt buckle.

"I've had five years to practice."

"I wish I had someone like you on my team."

"Mmm-hmmm," she said, leaning close to the mirror to apply mascara.

He cleared his throat. "In fact, I've been thinking a lot about that. We work really well together. I was wondering if I could get you to come to Greece with us and work on the doc for however long you have before production starts on your series. Even a couple of weeks would help. It'd be fun," he said persuasively.

Sabrina froze, the mascara brush hanging in the air. Back up, she ordered herself through the surge of adrenaline. He hadn't said what she'd just heard. He hadn't asked her to join him in his work, she thought in a simultaneous rush of panic and glee. For Stef, that was tantamount to a proposal. Once before he'd done that, she remembered, just before he'd broken her heart.

And it came over her in a rush of fear, how much deeper she was in than she'd been before. In college, she'd thrown herself into their relationship headfirst, but it had still only been first love. This time, she'd held back, kept up her guard, done everything she could to protect herself. For nothing. In risking herself before, she'd been hurt; in risking herself this time, she could be utterly destroyed. Anxiety choked her.

"Sabrina? Did you hear me?" Stef appeared at the door.

Sabrina jerked. "No, sorry, I was looking for something in my bag. What did you say?" She pushed the mascara wand into the tube, not wanting her shaking hands to show.

"I asked what you'd think about going to Greece with me for the shoot, just for a little while. I'd love to have you on our team." He paused. "I'd love a chance to be there with you."

Fear, trepidation, excitement mixed together until her stomach was roiling. Time, she thought, she just needed time to think. She could work it out.

STEF WATCHED SABRINA in the mirror as she met his eyes, then looked away, digging in her makeup bag.

"Well, I don't know how it would work out with the *True Sex* schedule," she hedged. "I couldn't make it for more than a few days to help you with the research."

It was that note in her voice that got to him. It was the tone she got sometimes when she was handling tricky details with a prickly person over the phone, that careful note that said she was talking slow and thinking a mile a minute while trying to be as cautious as possible. He'd seen and heard her do it a hundred times.

He'd never imagined she'd do it to him. And that it could hurt.

"Look, I just wanted to throw it out there. You don't have to answer now. Just think about it." He tapped the doorframe restlessly and paced a few steps out into the bedroom.

There was a small crash behind him. He was in the bathroom in an instant. "Are you okay?"

She'd dropped a pot of some sort of cosmetic that had spread crimson on the tile. "It slipped," she said, wiping up the mess, her hands shaking. "Clumsy of me. Look, it sounds like a great trip. It's just that you leave, when, in two weeks?"

"Two and a half. Friday after next," he said shortly.

She set the reddened hand towel aside. Slowly, she pulled out a lipstick and bent to the mirror. "There's…a lot going on right now. But I can look into schedules, see if I can work something out."

"Okay, Sabrina, I'm not a dog, you don't have to throw me a bone." Now frustration bloomed up to swamp the hurt. "If you don't want to come, just say so."

"Stef, I'm sorry."

Behind the smile, he saw a flash of strain, so quick that he could almost believe he'd imagined it. So quick he could almost believe it was what he wanted to see.

"I didn't mean to make it sound that way. I'm just surprised, that's all."

And afraid, he wondered, could that be it?

She came to him and pressed a soft kiss on his lips. "Honestly, I just need some time to think." Turning, she poked through her jewelry clutch on the counter and withdrew an amber and gold bracelet. "I think it would be fun, really. Here, help me with this," she asked, holding it out to him.

Now was not the moment to push, he told himself, looping the heavy square links around her wrist. Let her try the idea on for size, mull it over, and then she'd be ready to make a call. "Just think about it." He raised her fingers to his lips. "Take your time."

"WELCOME TO paradise," said a beautiful woman in a batik sarong, draping flower leis around their necks. They might have been standing in the convention center hallway, but the spirit of the islands filled the room in front of them. Everywhere they looked was a mass of color and fragrance, with squawking parrots perched in palm trees and steel drum music wrapping around all of it. Waiters in brightly flowered shirts circulated with drinks in hollowed-out pineapples and coconut shells.

Head To Paradise With Home Cinema read the banners overhead. A grandstand faced a movie-theater-sized screen along one wall. On a stage in front of it, a group of dancing girls in grass skirts did a hula.

Stef hooked a couple of coconut shells full of piña coladas off the tray of a passing waitress. "Looks kind of like my uncle Stavros," he said squinting at the fuzzy shell before handing one to her. A sudden surge of affection welled up in Sabrina at the sight of him, draped foolishly with flowers, sipping out of the shell with the little parasol pushed to one side.

She had to get somewhere quiet and think, just for a moment. Abruptly, she handed the shell back to Stef and gave him a quick kiss. "I'll be right back."

She stood at the little primping counter in the ladies' room and stared at her reflection in the mirror. When she and Stef had started sleeping together again, she'd consciously tried to avoid pinning down what it had meant. Sure, they'd laid the past to rest, but they'd steered carefully clear of anything to do with the future.

Now, it was as though he'd dropped a ticking box in her lap. It could be a fabulous gift like a diamond-encrusted watch.

Or it could be a bomb.

Come to Greece. It was more than just an invitation on a vacation junket, she knew. She knew what it meant.

What she didn't know was whether she could trust it. The irony was that as hard as she'd had to work to convince Stef that she'd changed, her biggest problem was suddenly being able to trust that he had. It seemed so, but knowing it and believing it were two different things when her heart was so deeply involved. Could she trust him, not just to mean what he said but to stand behind it?

And the real question, the deepest one, was what exactly did she feel for him? Her mind shied away from that into memories of the aftermath of their college affair. It was resolved, she reminded herself, and returned to the question. What did she feel for him, she asked herself, picking her way through the laughter and joys of the weeks just past, trying to find out what lay at the root of it all.

And anxiety rose up to choke her.

When she'd been a child, Sabrina had always been quick to climb the highest tree or to run laughing off the end of the high dive. And yet, when she thought of possibilities that Stef held out to her, fear she'd never felt before filled her.

But she'd dealt with fears before and forged ahead, not in spite of the fear but because of it. Because of the exhilaration of facing it and going onward. Because of the rewards she knew awaited.

So why, now, was she unable to make herself answer a simple question that her heart knew the answer to? When she thought of life without Stef in a month, how did she feel? And when she thought of herself five years in the future, whom did she see at her side?

And she knew. It was Stef, as simple as that. Nervous delight jittered in her stomach and she took a steadying breath. So she knew what she felt, which meant she maybe knew what she wanted. Now the question was how quickly could they finish with the reception so she could get him to herself and tell him?

SABRINA MADE HER WAY through the crowd to where Stef stood, watching a group of performers do the limbo.

"Having fun?" she asked.

"More than I can remember. How about you? Are you okay? You look a little flushed."

"I'm fine." She hooked her hand through his arm. "I ran into Royce Schuyler on my way back into the room. He wants us to be sitting where we can come up with the Candy girls when the clip airs. Come on, they're going to be starting the show soon."

They walked toward the grandstand area.

"Hey Sabrina, babe, give us a smile."

A flash blinded her and she stumbled momentarily. When the dazzle cleared from her eyes, she saw a familiar face behind the camera. Franzen, reporter for the *Weekly News*.

"The Creature from the Black Lagoon," she murmured.

"Come on, babe, stop and give me one."

"Who let a bottom-feeder like you in here, Franzen?"

He pointed to his press pass with a smug smile. "I guess they figure our readers want to know what you Hollywood types get up to. Want me to tell 'em, Sabrina?"

Stef tensed, but Sabrina caught his arm. "Don't give him any ammunition," she murmured as the camera flashed.

"Hey, I've got all the ammunition I need," Franzen leered obnoxiously. "So how've you and lover boy been?" he asked, following them toward the theatre.

"Bite me, Franzen," she said back.

As they reached their seats, the lights dimmed, the music came up with a flourish, and a dark-haired man with a suspiciously familiar face bounded onto the stage in a grass skirt.

"Is that—"

"David Beckley," Sabrina whispered back. "Sure is. He's got the top comedy show on Home Cinema, so I guess they figured they'd trot him out as MC. Just wait until the music starts and they have Britney do a tune."

"And to think, I was ready to give up all this just to stay back in the room and have wild sex in the hot tub."

"Can you believe how foolish you were?"

He squeezed her hand. "Yeah, I can."

"SMILE, YOU'RE SUPPOSED to be enjoying yourself."

Sabrina nudged Stef as they stood amid the mass of people in the ballroom. The presentations and the show were over. Now it was just a big, and progressively more drunken, party.

"Time of my life," Stef murmured, brushing a hand over her hair. "Isn't it time to go upstairs and wear ourselves out?"

"Soon," Sabrina laughed. "Work first, then play."

"This isn't still work, is it? You did your performance, you've done the meet and greet. Can't we go? I've got this insatiable urge to get you in a private place," he growled.

She grinned and then scooted out of his arms. "Come on, it's not like this is new to you. I mean, don't you do ShoWest?"

It was Stef's turn to laugh. "Theater execs go to ShoWest so they can take photos with Tom Cruise and Angelina Jolie, not so that they can meet some documentary film geek."

"An award-winning doc geek."

"Doesn't matter how many awards you've got, you don't spread the love like the stars."

"Well, look at it this way—this is the last one of these you'll have to go to."

"Hey." He caught her close for a moment. "If it's good for the doc and it's good for you, I don't mind doing it."

"We'll leave soon," she promised. "I just need to find Royce. He wanted to introduce me to a couple of the midwestern cable honchos. It's important, Stef." The look in her eyes pleaded with him to understand.

Stef sighed and followed her. She was like a fish, swimming happily in familiar waters. Running around a reception like this, doing the air kisses, being charming—she was in her element. For him, on the other hand, it was one long exercise in tedium. They needed to talk about what was going to happen, about their future, and instead she was flitting around with the president of North Centerville Cable.

No wonder it didn't excite her to think about going to Greece. Rural landscapes and ancient history weren't what she thrived on. What she thrived on was this: excitement, glamour, moving ahead and perhaps away from him if he didn't keep up. And keeping up wouldn't just be work, he thought, steeling himself for the next barrage of false cheer; it would be hard labor.

"Sabrina, just the person I was looking for." Schuyler slipped his arm around her shoulders. "Why don't you get some of your dancing friends over here and I can introduce you to John Chesterfield, head of cable operations in Omaha?"

Stef stood for a moment, ignored, watching Sabrina wave down the Candy contingent, and decided to head for the bar instead. He'd get a drink and find someplace to sit until she was done.

"Here you are, sir." The bartender handed him a Knob Creek and he swirled it around for a moment before taking the first swallow, letting the good Kentucky bourbon slide down his throat and into his veins. He stood out at the edge of the circle of activity, watching Mr. Omaha drape an arm around Sabrina's shoulders and squeeze, jostling her a bit with his drunken enthusiasm. Still, she gave him her best insincere company smile and said something that made him laugh. Stef knew it was her job, but annoyance pricked at him as he watched it. And the irrational, primitive part of him that already considered her his woman tightened at the scene.

"That Sabrina, she sure does get around."

Stef turned at the sound of the voice in his ear to see Franzen smirking at him.

Stef shook his head and turned back, ignoring him.

"Hey, it's a free country, I've got a press pass. I'm allowed to be here."

Across the room, Sabrina threw back her head and laughed at something one of the execs said. The exec who had his hand around her waist, now.

Franzen stepped closer to Stef, watching the scene with a little snigger. "Guess she didn't tell you when she took you on that you'd have to share, huh? Better drink up, buddy, it looks like it's going to be a long night before you get her to yourself."

Stef studied him for a moment the same way he'd

look at a scuttling cockroach. "Do yourself a favor, Franzen—shut up."

"You getting any from her?" Stef turned his head swiftly, and Franzen backed up a step. "Hey, I'm a reporter, just asking questions here."

"You're not reporting, Franzen—you're digging for sleaze." Stef shook his head and started away.

"You gotta know if you're banging Miss Party Girl over there, we're gonna be interested. The public's got a right to know. So, is she a good lay?"

Stef forced down the spurt of temper and kept walking.

"It's all right, Costas, you can tell me. 'Course, the way she's sticking her tongue down that guy's throat, maybe you should have her tested first."

Stef turned to see Mr. Omaha plant one on Sabrina.

"Get a shot of that," Franzen ordered his photographer. "We'll run it next to the pic of her mom crying and say it's a family embarrassment."

Stef raised his hand swiftly and put it over the lens. "That's enough."

The photographer cursed and tried to pull away, but Stef kept his hand on the lens.

"Goddammit, get your hands out of there," Franzen barked, shoving Stef. It had about as much effect as pushing a wall.

The photographer yanked at his camera again just as Franzen swiped at Stef's face.

It was reflex, that's what he'd tell himself later. It was a knee-jerk response to being attacked. It had to do with Franzen's hand coming at him, catching him along the cheekbone.

It had nothing to do with the sheer satisfaction of sending his fist up to Franzen's jaw in a pivoting right that had the snap of his entire body behind it.

Franzen's teeth clacked hard and his head snapped back. It felt, Stef thought as pain exploded up through his arm, glorious. And he watched Franzen crumple to the carpet.

19

WHEN IT CAME TO FIGHTS and hangovers, the morning after was seldom a pleasant experience. Stef stood at the sink in the room's dressing area and stuck his hand in the bucket of ice. He flexed the swollen knuckles, wincing. Uppercuts might be effective, but they were hard on the equipment. The last time he'd gotten into a fight, he'd been smart enough to go for a softer target—the nose.

He could still remember it—Denny Patterson, self-styled tough guy, pushing him up against the hallway wall. He'd rocked Denny back on his heels with a lucky punch, and blood had fountained everywhere. Of course, he'd paid for it with detention and a sworn enemy in Denny, but it had been worth it at the time.

Somehow, short-term gratification wasn't nearly so satisfying now that he was an adult.

The knock on the door startled him into the present.

"Room service." The knock on the door came again.

"I'll get it." The bathroom door opened and Sabrina came out swathed in a white terry robe with the hotel's logo stitched on it. She opened the door to the hall.

"Good morning," the waiter said, carrying the tray into the room. "Let's see, I've got coffee, juice and fruit here," he said, briefly raising the covers of the plates to show Sabrina. "Oh, and a copy of the local paper. If you'll just sign the slip?" he said, handing it to her. "Great. Have yourselves a lucky day."

Sabrina closed the door behind him and turned back to the stiff, tense atmosphere of the room. She walked over to Stef. "How's your hand?"

He piled some ice in a hand towel and folded it into an ice pack. "I'll live."

"Do you think we should get it looked at?"

"It'll be fine." He wrapped the pack around his hand, his words brusque.

Sabrina hesitated. "You know, you didn't want to talk about the fight last night. Maybe now would be a good time." She laid a hand on his back, but he just stiffened. Finally, she took her hand away and went to the room service tray and poured herself some coffee. She was setting the paper aside to reach for a strawberry when she glimpsed the front page and caught her breath.

"Let me guess," Stef said. "I've made the papers."

The National Cable Show claimed some prominent space, with a splashy story and lots of photos. And at the bottom was a sidebar, *Filmmaker Belts Journalist,* next to a shot of Stef punching Franzen.

Stef stiffened. "Jesus." He snatched the paper away from her. Short and pithy, the story traded maximum hype for minimal facts. It closed with a quote from Franzen threatening legal action.

"Great. Just what I need—a felony assault on my record." He tossed down the paper in disgust.

Sabrina stared at him. "How do you figure? He punched you first. It was hardly even a fight."

Frustration shouted from every ounce of his body. Stef stalked to the length of windows that made up one whole wall of the room. He stared out over the Vegas skyline. "I don't believe we're having this conversation," he said, almost to himself. "What the hell am I doing here?"

"It's just one of those things, Stef. It happens."

He whirled on her. "Not to me. I'll skip the juvenile theatrics, thanks. And I'll skip doing time in the tabloids."

"I hate to say it, but I don't think you're going to be able to avoid it." She cleared her throat. "Franzen holds a grudge. As a bonus, he knows he can get to me by getting to you, so it's going to be doubly sweet. I'd be careful what I throw out in the trash for the next six to eight months. I'm sorry," she said softly.

Stef turned back to the window and pressed his fingers to the glass. "This is not going to work," he said, his voice barely audible.

"Did you say something?" Sabrina raised her head.

"This is not going to work, Sabrina. It's just not."

Her lips felt cold. "What's not going to work?"

Stef stalked back to the bed. "This. Us. Hollywood." He snatched up the paper, smacking it with one hand. "I don't live the kind of life you lead. My investors sink money into my projects because they believe in the subject matter and they believe in me. They *don't* expect to see me showing up in the gossip column slugging a reporter, no matter how richly he might have deserved it."

"And what did he do to deserve it, by the way?" Sabrina rose from the bed and stepped toward him. "One minute everything was fine and the next thing I knew, Franzen was down." This wasn't happening, she told herself. It couldn't be happening all over again. She couldn't be listening to him and feeling this sickening lurch.

Stef cursed. "I can't believe this. I can't believe I let myself get caught up in this." He looked at her and then something seemed to crystallize for him. "Are you going to Greece with me or not?" he demanded.

The question caught her by surprise. The world seemed to be spinning in double time, too quickly for her to take it all in.

"I thought not," Stef snapped before she could answer, and stepped past her.

Sabrina wheeled on him. "Wait a minute. Is that what this is all about? That I didn't give you an answer last night in five minutes?"

He glared at her. "Yes, it's about Greece. It's about this," he said, holding up the paper, then flinging it to the bed. "It's about being in some tacky hotel room in Las Vegas so we can rub elbows with idiots who can't keep their hands off you. It's about being places I have no desire to be, doing things I don't want to do, just so I can be with you. And then when it's time to go somewhere you might not be comfortable, it's about having to hear…what? I don't know—you don't want to go, but you don't have the guts to tell me."

"But I can't just—"

"No, of course you can't. You have to stay here and make nice the Hollywood way. You want to know why

I slugged Franzen? To keep him from getting a shot of you with that conventioneer all over you."

"For God's sakes, it doesn't mean anything, Stef," she threw back at him, her eyes blazing. "Can't you get that through your head? The conventioneer doesn't matter and Franzen doesn't matter. I get hit by Franzen all the time, and I take my lumps. It's just part of doing business."

"He was going to put it on the cover and use that shot of your mother again. I saw your face when you told me about that one. I know what it does to you," he said furiously. "Is that what you call doing business? Well, I'm sorry, I can't. I can't let that happen to you, because to me it does mean something. And now I might be facing assault charges. I've got stories in the papers that may scare off any future funding. I've got an eighty-five-year-old grandmother who runs around her neighborhood bragging about her moviemaking grandson. How do you think she's going to feel when she walks into the grocery store and sees this? You want me to tell her it doesn't matter?"

Abruptly, his fury ebbed. "This is not my life, Sabrina. I can't live it. I love you, but I can't care about things and have you tell me they don't matter."

She froze. "What did you say?"

"I said I can't live this way."

"No, before that. Did you—"

He shook his head. "It doesn't matter." He pulled open the closet door and began pushing clothes into his carry-on. "You know, it's a good line, now that I think about it. That's what I'm going to start telling myself. It just doesn't matter, you know? It just doesn't matter."

And with his belongings hurriedly shoved into his bag, he walked out the door, leaving a stunned Sabrina behind him.

20

"HERE'S THE mail." Stef glanced up as Wendy, his administrative assistant, dropped a stack of items into his In box. "The courier brought your airline tickets, too."

Stef took the brightly colored envelope from her and stared at it. His tickets to Greece. There was a time he would have felt a little charge at what they presaged, but now he just tossed them into his travel folder and set it aside. So maybe some of the excitement was gone, but some of the excitement was gone out of just about everything these days. It was okay, he told himself.

It didn't matter.

In the past two weeks, the phrase had become his mantra. He said it when he went alone to the premiere of his union documentary and Franzen was there harassing him. He said it when he came across an anecdote only Sabrina would have appreciated but had no one to tell it to. Most of all, he said it when he woke in the night reaching for her and realized she wasn't there.

It didn't matter. In a little over twenty-four hours, he'd be flying to Greece and, once there, he'd have plenty to keep him occupied. Except, of course, for the one person he wanted.

It didn't matter.

Like he'd told Sabrina, it was a handy line. In the wasteland his life had become since Vegas, he'd been using it a lot. He was getting really good at it. And if he practiced it enough, maybe one of these days he might even believe it.

SABRINA SAT IN HER living room, watching the sunset along the canal. When the phone rang, she ignored it. The last thing she wanted to do was talk with anyone. Then the voice came out of the answering machine. "Hi, this is the Vandervere Detective Agency. I'm doing a missing persons search for Sabrina Pantolini. If you have any information, we—"

Sabrina smiled despite her mood and picked up the phone. "Hi, Kelly."

"You haven't been returning my calls, young lady. And you've been avoiding the Supper Club. We're starting to take it personally."

Sabrina let out a breath. "I'm sorry. Things are just hectic right now."

"Hey, I was just busting on you," Kelly said. "We're worried, that's all. I know the whole breakup with Stef was awful, but you don't have to go it alone. We're here if you need us."

"Thanks, Kelly. I just haven't felt much like being around people. Work is bad enough."

"Everything going okay, though?"

"Home Cinema bought the series."

Kelly whooped. "That's fabulous news."

"Yeah, life is good," Sabrina quipped and closed her

eyes. It was a ridiculous statement. Nothing was good, nothing at all. *Make an effort, dammit,* she told herself. "I got a director to work the rest of the *True Sex* series."

"Excellent. I know you were stressing over it." Kelly hesitated. "When do you start filming?"

"She can't start for a couple of weeks, which is good. I don't think I'd be ready for it right away."

"I'm so sorry, honey. If there's anything I can do…"

"It's okay. You've been great." Sabrina swallowed around the lump in her throat. "It's just one of those things that's going to take some time, you know? I guess it would be easier if I didn't feel like such a chump for letting the same thing happen to me twice."

"You went into it with the right intentions. It's not your fault that he let you down again."

"I just keep wondering if there was something we could have done differently."

"You'll drive yourself crazy with that one. Let it go."

"You're right," she sighed.

"I'm really sorry. I honestly thought things were going to work out this time."

Sabrina blinked rapidly, holding her breath until the urge to weep passed. She let out her breath slowly. "So did I. I guess we were both wrong."

"I know you probably don't want to hear that he's a waste of a human—"

"—being," Sabrina finished for her. "No, I don't really want to hear about him at all, just now, thanks. Listen, I got the copy of *Hot Ticket* with the article in it. It's really good, I mean it. I'd be saying that even if it weren't about my project. You're a great writer." She opened up the magazine and leaned back, leafing through it until she found Kelly's article.

And the opening shot, showing Stef behind the camera.

How could he not realize that they belonged together? How could he walk away over something so silly, blowing it all out of proportion. Was it really just a way of avoiding telling her that he didn't want her? How could he talk about her life being impossible for him without really saying that she was the one who was impossible? It made her want to break down.

"Are you still there?"

Sabrina started. "Yes, sorry, I was just flipping through the article."

"It got lead story. Hopefully you'll get a few more viewers for your premiere."

"It's great, Kelly, really."

"Hey, you want me to come over there? We can drink some wine, watch a movie…"

"Not right now, thanks. I think I'm going to just take a shower and call it a night. How about this weekend?"

Kelly coughed. "Um, can't do it. I'm going away."

"Good for you. Anyone I know?"

"Who do you think?"

Sabrina smiled. "I think you and young Mr. Cooper have been spending an awful lot of time together. Is this getting serious?"

"I don't know about that. It's fun, though, it really is…" Kelly's voice trailed off. "Oh, hell, I'm full of it. I'm in love with him."

"What?" Sabrina's eyes flew open in shock. "When?"

"A while ago. I didn't want to say anything while you were going through all this Stef stuff."

"Forget that. This is huge. I mean, you were the one who never wanted to get involved, and now…"

"I think people can change," Kelly said defensively. "You, of all people, should know that. It was that night at Cilla's party—it just hit me all at once."

Sabrina felt cold. "What's that?"

"That all the differences aren't important because it's what you are as a whole that matters. Once I figured that out, I knew what I needed to do." She cleared her throat in embarrassment. "Anyway, I don't want to go on about it. Listen, I'll call you Sunday night and maybe we can plan something for during the week."

"Okay. Hey, Kelly?"

"Yeah?"

"Don't feel that you can't tell me when something good is going on with you just because of this thing with Stef," Sabrina said gently. "I'm your friend. I want you to be happy."

"I want you to be happy, too."

"I will be," Sabrina said. *Maybe someday.*

MIDMORNING SUNLIGHT streamed in through the dirty window in Sabrina's office as she sat staring into space. It was the day Stef was leaving for Greece. Even now, he was probably heading for the airport to get on a plane and fly away from her, just as he'd already flown out of her life. She looked at her organizer where she'd scribbled his flight information, back in the days when she'd thought she'd be the one to see him off.

How had things gone so abysmally wrong? It had seemed like they'd finally understood each other, finally reached a place where they could come together. And then to have everything blow up over some idiotic move by Franzen… It was so unfair when it didn't *matter.*

It doesn't matter, she could hear Stef's voice. Why couldn't he see that Franzen didn't? Why couldn't he just let it go? Instead, he'd gotten hurt, gotten furious, torn apart something that was important over an incident that didn't mean anything.

Except to him.

Suddenly, she went shiveringly still.

It didn't matter to her, maybe, but it was crucial to him. It wasn't about him expecting her to relinquish her world and everything she was; it was about him expecting her to respect what was important to him. Respect what they were together.

All the differences aren't important because it's what you are as a whole that matters, Kelly had said. Sabrina's stomach tightened into a nervous knot. If they kept that clear in their minds, couldn't they use it to bridge the gaps between them? Couldn't they find a way to compromise, whether it was her doing less of the Hollywood whirl or him doing more? She solved problems daily in her job. There had to be a way to solve this one.

Sudden determination flooded over her. "Laeticia, I've got to leave." She shoved her chair back and stood up.

Laeticia looked up as Sabrina walked toward the outer office door. "Where are you going?"

"Greece."

At that instant, Laeticia proved herself worth a million. She didn't react, didn't waste time with questions, just looked at Sabrina calmly. "Right. What about a ticket?"

"I'll call my travel agent on the way to the airport. Postpone my appointment with Schuyler on Thursday and tell Gus we'll reschedule. I'll call the new director on my way to the airport." Sabrina gathered up her PalmPilot, notebook and a couple of the most critical files. "I'll call you when I know more about where I'll be and how long I'll be gone."

"You got a bag or you need me to send things for you?"

Sabrina smiled, feeling lighter with every passing minute. "What I need is at the airport."

STEF SAT IN THE departure lounge, leafing through his copy of *Hot Ticket*. It featured Kelly's story, he saw, flipping to the table of contents. That stopped him for a moment, the vivid memory of being on the set knowing that Sabrina was just a step or two away, that she'd be in his bed that night. It didn't matter, he reminded himself. He flipped to the article to test himself, to show himself that he could make it, and her, unimportant.

And he knew that he was full of it, because she wasn't unimportant.

She never had been.

Hollywood professes to love and admire the documentary, but that and a buck fifty will get you a cup of coffee. Perhaps it's because documentaries are sort of like vegetables—good for you, but not nearly as tasty as fries and burgers. Or, in the case of the moviegoing public, this month's teen comedy.

If Sabrina Pantolini has anything to say about it, though, you'll suddenly be finding documentaries as tasty as—

A voice came over the PA, interrupting his reading. "Ladies and gentlemen, welcome aboard our flight to Munich with continuing service to Athens. At this time we are boarding our first-class section. Passengers in rows one through six, welcome aboard."

Reluctantly, he closed the magazine and rose, slinging his carry-on over his shoulder. Normally, he'd have been in coach with the rest of the crew, but given that he was going out a week ahead of schedule, he'd decided to give himself a treat. Sabrina would have disapproved, he thought, before he could stop himself. But then again, she wasn't part of this project—or of his life—anymore.

And he had no idea how he was going to get used to that.

"How MANY BAGS are you checking?" the check-in agent asked, taking the signed charge slip from Sabrina.

"None," Sabrina said distractedly, glancing at her watch. "Am I going to make it?"

"It'll be close, but the security lines are better these days." The check-in agent stared at her computer screen, clicking some keys. "They've only just made the first boarding call, so you've got about half an hour. Good luck."

Sabrina dashed away from the counter, blessing her

travel agent for finding a way to shoehorn her onto the flight. She'd find Stef, and when she did, she'd convince him they'd find a way to make it work.

And if she couldn't convince him, at least she'd know she'd tried.

STEF SLOUCHED in his first-class seat, sipping the club soda the stewardess had brought him while reading Kelly's article. It was good, he realized. She had an uncanny knack for seeing right to the heart of the process…or the person.

> "I wanted to bring a slice of something different to general viewers," Pantolini says. "I wanted to show them that separate worlds aren't so different, that the people they think might be out on the fringes are a lot like you and me."

His heart squeezed painfully as he looked at a shot of Sabrina, her eyes alight in fun. How could anything have been important enough for him to walk away? He stared at himself in the same image—unsmiling, intent on the shoot. It didn't matter, he told himself.

> "Documentaries are about the discovery process," says director Stef Costas. "Sometimes it's about discovering a slice of life. Sometimes it's about discovering a part of yourself."

He stared at his words as the other passengers began to move down the aisle. Discovering a part of himself, the part of himself that was Sabrina.

The part of himself he'd torn away.

It didn't matter, he told himself fiercely. It didn't matter. And then suddenly, it was as though something tore within him. The hell with that. It did too matter. Sabrina mattered and he was not going to let her go without a fight.

Without thinking, he grabbed his carry-on and bolted up out of the seat.

"Sir, where are you going?" asked the flight attendant at the door.

"No checked luggage," he said, waving his ticket at her as he headed back up the Jetway.

At the door leading into the terminal, another agent stopped him. "Sir, I'm going to have to ask you to stop."

"What? I don't have checked luggage," he said, showing her his ticket folder.

"Security, sir. If you'll just step over to the central podium."

Stef stood, tapping his fingers impatiently. Now that he'd made the decision, all he could think about was getting to Sabrina and convincing her to come with him.

Fat chance, Costas, he thought with a snort. He'd figure out a way, though, he realized. They'd figure out a way. Even if it meant a relationship conducted by cell phones and e-mail for a few months, they'd do it. She had a career that he respected; no way would he expect her just to drop everything.

But maybe she was through with him after the boneheaded way he'd behaved. It was entirely possible.

So what, he told himself, shaking his head. He'd get around it, somehow, some way.

When the gate agent looked up and nodded at him, he breathed a sigh of relief and headed toward the main concourse. He'd find her. He'd track her down, whether he had to go to her office or her home or crash a meeting. He'd even walk into a shoot if he had to.

Because it mattered.

SABRINA SET HER BAG on the belt of the X-ray machine and hurried through the metal detector. Though her watch said it had only been five minutes, the line had seemed to take forever. There was a plane out there with a seat with her name on it and she wasn't going to miss it.

She snatched up her belt and her bag off the conveyor, not bothering to put her belt back on. Later, she thought. Once she was on the plane, she could primp to her heart's content. For now, the two minutes it might take to thread it through her loops were two minutes she couldn't afford.

Slinging the bag over her shoulder, she began hurrying down the broad corridor that led toward the gates, her heels tapping impatiently against the terrazzo floor. She dodged and weaved, trying to work her way around the masses of rush-hour airport traffic as she headed toward a gate that was, naturally, at the farthest end of the terminal.

Then she saw the solid mob of people ahead of her and she cursed again.

"OKAY, I'VE GOT EVERYONE'S boarding passes and passports," the harried-looking woman shouted to the mass of teenagers standing around her. She struggled to be heard over the hubbub from the milling crowd. Some kind of a school trip, Stef thought, wishing to hell she'd been smart enough to gather them all together somewhere besides the narrowest part of the concourse.

He moved to the right trying to skirt them—as was, unfortunately, every other traveler going his way. Teenagers were definitely getting taller these days, not to mention wider, and when you packed a couple hundred of them together, well, it made for one hell of an obstacle.

Stef weaved his way impatiently through them. Now that he knew what he needed to do, he didn't want to waste a minute getting to Sabrina. He wanted to see her, he wanted to hear her. He wanted her in his arms.

There was a shout and a crash as one of the kids leaned against a freestanding metal sign in front of a snack bar, knocking it over and in the process knocking a drink from a bystander's hands. Stef looked over in reflex.

And he saw her.

For a moment, everything went still. Someone banged into him from behind, but he didn't care. The only thing he cared about was Sabrina. She just stared at him, her eyes enormous. He didn't think to wonder what she was doing there. It was as though his prayers had been answered and all he could feel was stupidly grateful that he had been given another chance.

SHE HAD TO BE dreaming. It couldn't be Stef. He should be sitting on a plane. Her pulse hammered high in her throat. Move, she told her legs, but they stayed frozen. All she could do was watch him as he crossed the concourse to her.

"You're going to miss your flight," she said faintly.

He shook his head. "I already got off it. What are you doing here?"

She swallowed and raised her chin. "I came to find you."

"You bought a ticket to get behind security so you could talk to me?"

"I bought a ticket to go to Athens."

He opened his mouth, but no sound came out.

"Look," she said desperately. "I thought about it and it took me a while but I realized I was wrong the other day, to tell you that stuff wasn't important, okay? I know that now." Her eyes stung and she blinked rapidly. "And I know we come from different worlds, but they're not that different. We can make this work, if we want to. And if that means that I give something up or you give something up, that's okay, right? That's what people do when they love each other. You make it work. You make it matter." The tears were slipping down her cheeks now, but she didn't care.

Stef just stared at her and her heart thundered in her ears. *Say something,* she thought, *say something.*

Instead, he pulled her shaking body to him and squeezed. "My God, Sabrina, my God, my God," he said softly, while she breathed in the scent of him and gloried in the feel of his arms around her. "I've been walking around for two solid weeks telling myself that it was all right, that I'd done the right thing, that it didn't matter that you were gone. I kept thinking it would get better, but it didn't. It just got worse." He loosened his arms.

"You mean everything to me, Stef," Sabrina told him. "I couldn't stand to lose you."

"I was the one who was wrong. You talk about what people do when they love each other, well they don't sit and berate the other person because God forbid, they have to spend one night doing something they don't want to." He put his hands on her shoulders and looked at her. "They talk, they compromise. Like we're going to do."

"I love you so much, Stef."

An announcement from a nearby gate startled them both. "Looks like the traffic jam has cleared. We'd better get out of the way," Stef said.

"What we'd better do is get to our gate," Sabrina said.

"You sure you can get away?" He looked at her intently.

"Absolutely, at least for a while. You think I want to be apart from you now? It's going to be hard enough being separated during the flight while I'm back in coach."

"Well, I don't think we necessarily have to be separated," Stef said slowly.

"First class is sold out. I checked."

"That's okay. I'm betting the person next to you in coach would be happy to trade for my first-class seat."

She tilted her head. "You'd give up first class for me?"

"I'd give up anything for you. I meant what I said before. We're going to find a way to make this work." Then he leaned forward to press a tender kiss on her forehead. "Because it matters."

* * * * *

Don't miss the next instalment of the
SEX & THE SUPPER CLUB
from the award-winnng author
Kristin Hardy…

Next up: Trish's story – Cutting Loose.
Coming next month!

MILLS & BOON®

Live the emotion

Blaze™

CUTTING LOOSE by Kristin Hardy

Sex & the Supper Club

A makeover. A masked stranger. A master suite. When Trish Dawson's new look attracts the attention of a fellow party guest, she decides to cut loose and go for it. When the mask comes off, not to mention his clothes, actor Ty Ramsay is revealed. Will this be a one-night only performance?

HARD TO HANDLE by Jamie Denton

Lock & Key

Successful lawyer Mikki Correlli has worked hard to achieve the perfect life. When she attends a "lock and key" party, she hopes to have some sexy fun, no strings attached. What she doesn't expect is to run into Nolan Baylor – her ex-husband.

VIRTUALLY PERFECT by Samantha Hunter

Raine Covington has found the perfect lover – online. When Jack's sexy words fly across the computer screen, he can seduce her in a heartbeat. So why is she feeling unsatisfied? Once Raine and Jack meet face-to-face, both are surprised at the outcome…

BARED by Jill Shalvis

Emma Willis never expects to find herself wearing next to nothing and posing for a sexy calendar, but she can't refuse her twin sister's request for help. All Emma has to do is follow the photographer's instructions. Easier said than done once she catches sight of the sexy photographer Rafe Delacantro.

On sale 3rd February 2006

Available at WHSmith, Tesco, ASDA, Borders, Eason, Sainsbury's and most bookshops

www.millsandboon.co.uk

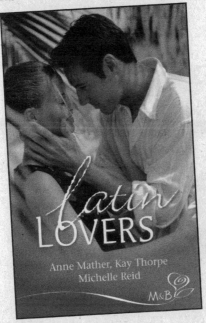

Three fabulous stories from popular authors Anne Mather, Kay Thorpe and Michelle Reid bring you passion, glamour and pulse-raising Latin rhythm and fire.

On sale 3rd February 2006

Available at WH Smith, Tesco, ASDA, Borders, Eason, Sainsbury's and all good paperback bookshops

www.millsandboon.co.uk

2 FREE

BOOKS AND A SURPRISE GIFT!

We would like to take this opportunity to thank you for reading this Mills & Boon® book by offering you the chance to take TWO more specially selected titles from the Blaze™ series absolutely FREE! We're also making this offer to introduce you to the benefits of the Reader Service™—

- ★ **FREE home delivery**
- ★ **FREE gifts and competitions**
- ★ **FREE monthly Newsletter**
- ★ **Exclusive Reader Service offers**
- ★ **Books available before they're in the shops**

Accepting these FREE books and gift places you under no obligation to buy, you may cancel at any time, even after receiving your free shipment. Simply complete your details below and return the entire page to the address below. You don't even need a stamp!

YES! Please send me 2 free Blaze books and a surprise gift. I understand that unless you hear from me, I will receive 4 superb new titles every month for just £3.05 each, postage and packing free. I am under no obligation to purchase any books and may cancel my subscription at any time. The free books and gift will be mine to keep in any case.

K6ZED

Ms/Mrs/Miss/Mr ....Initials ....

BLOCK CAPITALS PLEASE

Surname ....

Address ....

....

....Postcode..

Send this whole page to:
UK: FREEPOST CN81, Croydon, CR9 3WZ